All thoughts of resistance, every scrap of pride disappeared as his mouth invaded hers.

He did desire her! His past actions, his seeming indifference, had appeared to deny it, but now the walls were down. The old magic was back with a vengeance, a force stronger than both of them combined.

Blind emotion claimed her as her mouth answered his raw passion, greedy fingers curving into the luxurious thickness of his dark-as-night silky hair as the heat of his arousal, hard against her yielding softness, turned her into a delirious wreck.

With a smothered, wickedly sexy groan, Ettore held her slightly away from him, his hooded eyes magnetic, holding her in thrall as they very thoroughly slid like a caress over her unashamed nakedness.

"I burn for you, my Sophie," he breathed on a driven undertone. "Come to me?"

Mama Mia!

Harlequin Presents®

ITALIAN HUSBANDS

They're tall, dark...and ready to marry!

If you love marriage of convenience stories that ignite into marriages of passion, then look no further. We've got the heroes you love to read about and the women who tame them.

Watch for more exciting tales of romance, Italian-style!

Available only from Harlequin Presents®!

Diana Hamilton

THE ITALIAN'S MARRIAGE DEMAND

ITALIAN HUSBANDS

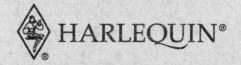

HARLEQUIN®

TORONTO • NEW YORK • LONDON
AMSTERDAM • PARIS • SYDNEY • HAMBURG
STOCKHOLM • ATHENS • TOKYO • MILAN • MADRID
PRAGUE • WARSAW • BUDAPEST • AUCKLAND

ISBN 0-373-12491-0

THE ITALIAN'S MARRIAGE DEMAND

First North American Publication 2005.

Copyright © 2005 by Diana Hamilton.

www.eHarlequin.com

Printed in U.S.A.

CHAPTER ONE

'WELL, thanks a bunch!' Sophie directed a ferocious hiss at the tail-lights of the lorry which had drenched her and the antiquated pram with a breath-snatching spray of icy rainwater. Frustration and growing anxiety tightened her delicate jawline. If she didn't get across this wretched road in the next few minutes she was going to be late getting to the address in Finsbury Circus.

Last night, in response to her frantic phone call, when Tim had agreed to give her a roof over her head just until she'd got herself sorted out, he'd stressed that he would only have a half-hour window in his lunchbreak to let her into his flat. Already there was a scant fifteen minutes of that time remaining.

Sophie's temperature rose another few hectic degrees. If Nanny Hopkins's landlord hadn't been late turning up to collect the key and the final week's rent she would have made it to Tim's flat with time to spare. But now—

Poised to take advantage of any gap in the traffic, she took a deep breath and made herself remember that dear old lady's firm stricture when things, as they usually did for her, went drastically wrong to 'look on the bright side, child. You'll always find one'.

Nanny Hopkins's little homilies had always been predictable, but were almost always dead right. So

Sophie made a conscious effort to relax her tense shoulders and remind herself that things weren't all bad. At least her sleeping seven-month-old son and their possessions were dry beneath the capacious hood and apron of the ancient contraption that would have caused passers-by to cast superior stares in her direction if scurrying through the murk and rain of the gloomy late-January day hadn't preoccupied them.

And if Tim had to give up on her—mindful of his hopes of promotion to manager of the travel agency—then she could always find a modest café where she and her baby would be warm and dry, and nurse a cup of tea until Tim was due to return in the evening. No problem—well, not a huge one. The great thing was she and her son had somewhere to stay while she looked for employment and she wouldn't have to go cap in hand to Social Services.

Hopes of spotting a break in the constant stream of traffic were now fading to non-existence. She would have to trudge further down the street and hope providence would provide a pedestrian crossing. Fuming at the enforced lengthening of her journey when minutes were ticking by, Sophie tightened her grip on the push bar and heaved the unwieldy pram around to face the new direction—and found progress blocked by an unquestionably solid lamp-post.

Compressing her lush pink lips, she struggled to make the necessary reverse-press-on-manoeuvre, slipped backwards off the edge of the kerb in haste and landed in the gutter in a miserable, undignified heap, with the screech of brakes in her ears and the bumper of a sleek silver car just a fraction of an inch from her shock-whitened face.

She could have been killed, as well as being homeless and as near-as-dammit destitute! Then what would have happened to her darling baby? A huge hot sob filled her throat. It didn't bear thinking about! Why was she such an idiot? As a mother and provider she would give herself nil out of ten—and that was being overly generous.

Ettore Severini swung the hired silver Mercedes into the traffic heading out of Threadneedle Street and into Bishopsgate with decisive panache. Business meetings for today had been completed as satisfactorily as expected. As always.

He had the afternoon free, apart from looking through some paperwork. Then two more days here in London, on one of his regular visits—two days packed with more scheduled meetings—then back to Florence, back to base. To an early spring. Probably a false spring. But no matter. To be out of the seemingly perpetual gloom of this rain-soaked, cloud-oppressed city would be a relief.

Five days of intense negotiations, business dinners, board meetings and sessions of stamping his authority around the London headquarters of the Severini family bank had failed to give him the expected surge of satisfaction of work well done. Signally and strangely failed today.

He felt...not tired—he was never tired; his stamina was legendary—what? Empty? As if an elusive something was missing in his gold-plated life. A frown pulled level ebony brows down, narrowing his coolly brilliant dark eyes. He despised negative introspection. Refused to waste time indulging in the stuff!

Madonna diavola! Didn't he have everything a guy could ask for? Thirty-six years old, with his health and strength, wealth beyond the dreams of avarice and, since his father's death four years ago, the undisputed driving force behind his family's long-established merchant bank. He had even—to his wry amusement—been recently described in one of the more sober broadsheets as a financial genius. Plus, he had his pick of beautiful women—when he could be bothered to take up their overt invitations—and a fiancée who was happy to turn a blind eye and was as laid-back as he was about setting the date for what would be a purely dynastic marriage.

A lifestyle any red-blooded male would envy. So what the hell could be missing?

Not one single thing!

Back at the Severini London apartment he would shower, open a bottle of Brunello di Montalcino, listen to music—Verdi? Yes, definitely—and let the rich red wine transport him back to Tuscany, to cypress shadows banding hot white roads, the cool green reaches of the Apennines, olive groves, the drowsy hum of bees in the wild herbs. The odd, discontent that had no name would be entirely banished.

His strong yet finely made hands relaxed on the wheel. The traffic was horrendous. The wipers rhythmically handled the murky drizzle, and the greasy spray thrown up by other vehicles. It would depress anyone who let it.

Another depressing sight was a few dozen yards

ahead—one of the unfortunates. A bag-lady bunched up in some sort of raincoat, an old woolly hat pulled down over her head, struggling with an ancient pram that undoubtedly held her meagre possessions. He supposed it was a 'her'. It looked too short and round to be a guy.

Traffic was moving at a steady, if frustrating ten miles an hour. Drawing almost level with the tussle on the pavement, Ettore stamped on the brakes as the disreputable figure toppled backward, landing in an ungainly heap just beneath the sleek silver bonnet.

Cursing through suddenly colourless flattened lips, Ettore exited the car in one driven movement, oblivious of the traffic, the blaring of horns. Had he hit the pathetic creature? He didn't think so. He would have felt the impact. Nevertheless...

Long, rapid strides propelled him around the front of the car. She was still sitting where she'd landed, in the gutter with all the other discarded rubbish, her back towards him, head downbent. A lock of long, rain-darkened blonde hair escaped the sodden woollen hat. Definitely female.

As he reached out a hand to gently touch the back of her hunched shoulder he demanded, 'Are you hurt?' and she shot to her feet as if a bomb had exploded beneath her, lurching forward towards the stranded pram.

A small crowd of onlookers had gathered, but, seeing the victim on her feet and shooting forward with energy, lost interest, remembered the now driving rain and drifted away.

'Wait.' If he was right and the woman was one of the city's homeless—and appearances suggested that was the case—then the least he could do was offer her the price of a good meal and a bed for the night. Make sure she was okay. 'You've had a shock.'

Both hands firmly on her shoulders, he swung her round, mentally calculating how much sterling he had in his wallet. A couple of hundred or so. Adequate compensation?

His faint frown developed into a full-blown black scowl as her pale-as-skimmed-milk face lifted to his. His heart gave an almighty, totally sickening thump. *Dio mio!*

His voice was an icy bite when he finally got out, 'Sophie Lang, by all that's unholy! Down and out in the gutter, where you belong!'

Ettore regretted the scathing words as soon as they'd spilled out between grindingly clenched teeth. Insulting the wretched woman was both undignified and a waste of breath. And what did that instinctive, ill-considered outburst say about him? That he still cared that the lovely, caring, warm and incredibly sexy woman who had bewitched and beguiled him had turned out to be a scheming little thief?

Of course he didn't care! How could he? He'd sliced her out of his heart and his head with surgical precision, well over a year ago. Written the whole unsavoury business off as valuable experience.

Sophie couldn't have said a word if her life had depended on it. A moment ago a hand on her shoulder, a voice saying something, had galvanised her out of the immobility of shock. But now every scrap of energy had drained right out of her again, leaving her as limp as a lump of over-boiled cabbage.

Him! Here in London! The very last man she

wanted to see, to have to admit back into a mind that had finally wiped him from her memory banks. As savagely handsome as ever, with raindrops sparkling against that superbly cut, soft as silk night-black hair and a mouth that promised and delivered heaven on earth—a mouth to die for. Expensively classy tailoring clothed his honed, blow-your-mind-sexy six-foot physique with fluid Italian elegance, and the impressively beautiful package was toughened by the reluctantly remembered quality of intimidating detachment that could be turned on at will.

She could barely breathe beneath that now dismissive stare, her face flaming with fiery colour then immediately whitening.

Her wide grey eyes looked haunted, Ettore noted dispassionately, ringed by dark circles and entirely dominating her ashen features. Her soft unpainted mouth was quivering. The shock of a near accident? Or something else? She was obviously unharmed.

Uttering a curse beneath his breath, Ettore told himself that the way she looked was of no possible interest to him. If she was down and out, maybe even recently released from prison—not all her victims would be as generous as he had been—then she only had herself to blame.

With that common sense thought in mind, he was turning away when a rageful squawk issued from the depths of the unspeakably dreadful pram. His brows lowering, he watched as Sophie leant over and extracted a soft shawl-wrapped bundle and cradled it against her heart. The tender, loving expression that suffused her features momentarily recaptured the inner beauty that had once so entranced him. But then she had impressed him by treating Flavia's twins not only firmly but as if they were the most precious and special children to walk the earth.

An excellent nanny. Reluctantly, he couldn't fault her on that. And working through a highly respected UK agency, which meant that she was still successfully duping everyone around her, which in turn brought on his terse, 'Surely your present employers can afford to supply your charge with a more up-to-date conveyance? It looks as if it was found on a skip.'

He rocked back on his heels, his hands thrust deep into the pockets of his fine cashmere overcoat, one ebony brow raised. The tightly swaddled child was settled now, blowing burbling bubbles into the side of her neck.

He watched Sophie's cute triangular face pinken, the dark, blonde-tipped lashes veiling her eyes as she countered woodenly, 'I no longer work. As a nanny. A fact I'm sure you're perfectly aware of, *signor.*' The stress on the formal mode of address was slight but unmistakeable. 'Torry is my son.'

And yours, she mentally added. Nothing would induce her to say the words aloud. Wild horses wouldn't drag them from her!

'And now—' she made an economical movement towards the pram, tension pulling a line between her eyes '—I have to go. I'm already very late.'

'Where to?'

A mean wind was gusting now, and the rain was falling more heavily, blowing horizontally. Her face was thinner than he remembered it. Pale. On the island her skin had glowed with health, with the touch of the sun, and she'd had a charming band of light freckles across the narrow bridge of her neat nose. A nose that wrinkled when she laughed and sometimes even when she simply smiled.

She had smiled a lot. Her unfeigned, uncomplicated *joie de vivre* had been the first thing to draw him into her web. With hindsight he accepted that her warmth and lightness of spirit had been some of the tools in her impressive armoury. That armoury had to be five-star-rated, he conceded bitterly, to have bamboozled a cynically sophisticated hard-nosed banker, turning a life that had been planned with mathematical precision on its head.

She was ignoring him, bending over the pram, doing her best to shield the wriggling child from the rain while folding back the waterproof apron.

Irritated with her lack of response to a perfectly reasonable question, and even more irritated with himself for caring one way or another, he loomed over her. 'Well?'

Why couldn't he just go away? Sophie felt like screaming. Seeing him again was turning her into a mental wreck. She'd forced herself to forget. Wipe out the memory of those magical weeks on the island, of the way they had been, the way she'd loved him and fooled herself into believing he'd loved her. And the aftermath. A nightmare filled with humiliation, pain and cringe-making disgrace. His willingness to believe she was a thief, his icy indifference to her flustered denial, the way he'd made very sure she never worked as a nanny again.

'Finsbury Circus,' she muttered, stiff-jawed. If she answered his question—although he had no business asking it in the first place—then he just might re-move his unwanted presence and she could get a real move on. She sagged defeatedly.

No use hurrying. By the time she got there Tim would have left. He wouldn't want to be late back for work, not while promotion was in the offing. And the taxi crammed with the rest of her gear wasn't due to arrive until early evening—at Tim's sugges-tion. Apparently there were stairs, lots of them, and she'd need a hand getting the bulkier stuff to his second-floor flat.

'I'll drive you. It's no distance.' Not a suggestion. More of a tersely delivered command.

'No.' She'd walk until her feet dropped off rather than accept a lift from him.

'Don't be an idiot,' he gritted with deep impa-tience. 'You're soaking wet and on your own admis-sion you're incapable of keeping your appointment under your own steam.'

He already had her arm in an unbreakable grip, steering her reluctant frame towards the illegally parked silver car. He had the passenger door open. The leather seat looked inviting. The interior was blessedly warm and dry. But there was the lingering fragrance of the aftershave he favoured. It was too—too intimate. He wouldn't feel it, of course. He deeply despised her. He wouldn't demean his exalted person by feeling a resurgence of that wild craving that had catapulted them into a passionate affair, en-slaving her utterly. But, hatefully, she did. She couldn't bear it!

Her insides in a knot, Sophie dug her heels in. 'My pram! I can't just leave it—it's got all my stuff—'

'I'll deal with it. Stop wasting my time and yours. Just get in.'

It was delivered in the authoritative tone of a man who called all the shots. Sophie fulminated as Torry stiffened in her arms. They could stand out here in this vile weather arguing the toss all day, and she had her baby's welfare to think about. That came streets ahead of her need for total independence as far as Ettore Severini was concerned.

Flags of bright colour flashed across the delicate arch of her cheekbones as she reluctantly capitulated, obeying his bitten instruction to 'belt yourself and the child in' as he strode over to the pram and pushed it across the glistening pavement towards a charity shop.

It took only seconds, and a generous donation, to offload the hideous thing and extract soft woolly blankets, a furry blue teddy bear and assorted bulging carriers from the cavernous depths. Ettore didn't know why he was bothering. Not for the sake of that sly, thieving minx, that was for sure!

He was bothering for the sake of the poor, innocent kid. Yes, of course. Pleased with that solution to his admittedly bizarre behaviour, he dumped the contents of the pram on the rear seat and slid behind the wheel. No wife of his would be forced to venture out in such weather, pushing a child around in something that might have been in fashion when Queen Victoria was on the throne.

His teeth set. Perhaps they couldn't afford anything better?

'Address?' he gritted, firing the engine.

Absorbing her snippily delivered reply, he eased

out into the traffic. She was wearing no wedding ring. Single mother? She must have gone straight from his bed into another's! His insides gave an angry twist.

The baby gurgled. Blew a loud raspberry. A swift sideways glance revealed plump arms vigorously waving, the woolly bonnet thing riding high on his head revealed a mass of glossy dark curls. Curls as dark and shiny as his big brown eyes. Cute kid! Pity the poor thing was landed with a promiscuous thief for a mother.

Peering at the digital clock on the dashboard, Sophie reckoned they might make it. Just. Concentrate on that, she drilled firmly into her head, willing herself to stop mourning over the fact that she looked such an awful fright. Like a bloated whale!

The pile of her possessions—baby stuff that now cluttered up the hallway of Nanny Hopkins's kindly neighbour, waiting for collection—would have to be shoehorned into the taxi as it was, without adding a binbag full of her own clothing. Spare space in the pram had been taken up with Torry's essentials— nappies, changes of clothing, bottles of formula that only needed heating, packets of rusks—so she'd had no option but to wear everything she owned, covering up with the voluminous old raincoat Nanny Hopkins used for tending her beloved back garden in poor weather.

So, okay, she looked absolutely dreadful. It couldn't matter less, could it?

'So what's this appointment? Business or personal?' Ettore asked, simply for something to say to break through the taut wall of silence that was blistering his eardrums. Not because he was interested. No way. He'd taken it on himself to get her kid out of the vile weather and he'd prefer the short journey to be a little less uncomfortable.

'Personal.' Nervous tension made her voice thin and squeaky.

Ettore's gaze slid in her direction. His brow lowered. She looked ill. Pale. Her face was thinner than it should be, with perspiration glistening on her forehead and short upper lip. Yet her body was undeniably overweight, the former fantastic curves and delectable indentations lost in bloated shapelessness.

'And?' he bit out. Too harshly? What in the name of all that was sacred was the matter with him? He didn't give a toss about her personal arrangements! Indicating, he swung the car into a relatively traffic-free street, slowing, searching for the number she'd given.

He heard her sigh. Then, in an irritated rush, 'I'm moving in with a friend. He's only got a limited amount of time to hang around to let me in.' She pushed the words at him—anything to get him off her case. 'He might already have given up on me.'

But he hadn't. Sophie's heart gave a huge jerk of relief as Tim bounded down the short flight of steps that led to the street door of the tall terraced house as Ettore braked to a halt outside the looked-for address.

Exiting as Sophie all but scrambled out of the car, clinging onto her wide-awake and wide-eyed son, Ettore reached for the stuff he'd bundled onto the back seat. Was this the baby's father? She'd said she was moving in with him. Had he belatedly accepted his responsibilities? For the kid's sake, he'd feel easier if he believed that.

Eyes narrowed, he watched the guy. He didn't look the dependable type. Tall and gangly, blond hair all over the place, pale blue eyes, as fair as Sophie was. Not likely to be the baby's father. His temperature rose. How many guys did she run through? Not that he cared, of course. Just thanked heaven for the lucky escape he'd had.

Her new guy was talking quickly, pressing something into Sophie's free hand, jerking his head back towards the house. Then, after dropping a swift kiss on her upturned cheek, he was off, heading down the street, uncoordinated long legs covering the pavement at speed, his unbelted trench coat ballooning out behind him.

Sorted. She and her kid would be out of the rain in seconds. So why wasn't he feeling comfortable with that? Wide shoulders lifted in a minimal shrug beneath the smooth cashmere before he wrote the aberration off as inconsequential and strode towards her. 'Everything all right?'

She mumbled something inaudible, willing him to go away, leave her alone. She hated the way he made her pulses leap, the way she loathed him for what he'd turned out to be, for what he'd done to her, yet couldn't stop herself remembering the heat of his passion, the hauntingly vivid memories she'd thought she'd blocked out for ever. She mounted the steps at what she hoped was a dignified pace, the backs of her knees prickling because she knew he was following.

Opening the back door onto a narrow barren hallway, she stepped inside and said, with ultra-politeness, 'Thank you for the lift.' She didn't look at him. Her mouth ran dry. She just couldn't! She just indicated the blankets and carriers he was holding. 'Leave them here. I'll come down and collect them later.' And turned for the stairs.

Torry was starting to grizzle. She held him closer to her over-padded body. She didn't want him drawing attention to himself. Ettore was no fool. She didn't want her baby's physical characteristics to start wheels turning in that clever Severini brain!

She heard him following. Still following! He had no right—she didn't want him near her or her baby. He had forfeited any rights he had in that context when he'd branded her as a thief and made sure she would never be employed as a nanny again!

Recognising the waves of heat banging inside her brain as incipient hysteria, she dragged in a deep, albeit shaky breath and tried to cool it. Pointless to throw a hissy fit over something as mundane as mere politeness.

His inherent good manners had impressed her on first meeting him at his sister and brother-in-law's timelessly elegant home in Florence. He'd treated her, the stop-gap nanny, only there while the permanent holder of that plum position had been recovering from a broken leg, as if she were a valued guest. So, even though he had her marked as a common thief, that inbred politeness wouldn't allow him to walk away and see her carry the bulky belongings up two flights of stairs.

Even so—she bit down hard on the soft flesh of

her lower lip as her wobbly fingers inserted the key in the lock of the door plainly marked with Tim's name—he was so close now. His nearness was practically blistering her skin. Could he sense how her pulse rate scampered? Her breath was coming in shallow gasps, all the old primitive responses well and truly triggered, assailing her body every which way there was! It was loathsome and horribly demeaning to accept that her body still reacted to him when she hated him with both her head and her heart.

'Thank you.' And how she managed even those two thin, bitten-off words she would never know. She was wound up to the point of explosion. She'd meant no more to this privileged, exalted being than a furtive holiday fling.

Her world had fallen apart when that unsavoury, deeply humiliating fact had hit her right between the eyes. That he'd believed the word of that upper-class, superior snob Cinzia di Barsini above her flustered rebuttal had left her feeling bitterly hurt, rejected and broken-hearted. The fact that he'd gone on to deny her the career she loved had added deep resentment to the mix.

The door opened directly onto the living area. Typical bachelor pad, the only concession to creature comforts was a vast leather-covered sofa in front of a state-of-the-art flatscreen TV, and a low side table sporting a couple of empty beer cans. How Ettore, used to discreet luxury and priceless antiques, a feather-bedded existence, would view the drab featureless walls, the piles of old motoring magazines stuffed in one corner of the low-ceilinged attic room, was a given.

'Goodbye.' Sticking to formality was the only way she could handle this. She half turned towards him, watching as he placed her belongings on the sofa. But dignity was difficult to maintain when Torry had grabbed her woolly hat with one determined little fist and was dragging it down over her eyes, and she was horribly sure that her disintegrating ponytail would be sticking out at the back.

Ettore's dark eyes were on her now. Pitying? Sophie's chin came up as she fought for cool.

'You've been—' a struggle to get the words out '—very kind.' Nosy, more like. Wondering to what depths the thieving little slapper who had briefly spiced up the tedium of a duty visit to the island had sunk! Willing her thumping heart to settle down, she turned to practicalities. 'Did you ask when it would be convenient for me to collect my pram?'

If the charity shop wouldn't store it beyond today it would mean another trek in the rain, toting Torry. Though the arrogant brute wouldn't have thought of that, would he?

One dark brow lifted, and the beautiful mouth quirked at one corner. If she'd been feeling generous Sophie might have attributed it to slight amusement.

She wasn't. The suspicion that he was presenting her with a very superior sneer was doubly confirmed when he stated, 'You don't. I donated it to the charity.' Plus a generous cheque for any trouble they might have in getting it into the nearest skip. But, to spare any lingering sensibilities she might still possess, he held his tongue on that slice of information.

Ettore slid a hand into his breast pocket, the movement stilling as Sophie finally lost it.

'How dare you?' Grey eyes glistened with tears of rage. 'You had no right to give my property away! It had sentimental value!' Her chest heaved with a hot mixture of anger and anguish as she vividly recalled the day when Nanny Hopkins had proudly wheeled the pram down the street. She'd acquired it through an acquaintance who worked for a titled old lady who resided in Belgravia. It had been in the attic for decades, and Lady Gore-Blenchley had been only too pleased to learn that it would be going to a good home.

'Just think of the aristocratic little boys and girls who've taken their daily airings in it.' Nanny Hopkins had beamed, pleased as punch. 'They don't make them like this any more. This is quality. See how beautifully sprung it is! Give me an hour and it will come up like new. It will be perfect for when your precious little baby arrives.'

Heavily pregnant, Sophie had had her doubts. But she wouldn't have let them show for all the tea in China.

The gentle elderly lady had been her rock for all of her twenty-four years. After she'd been dismissed from her post when Sophie's father had remarried after her own mother's early death Nanny had kept in touch, writing long, upbeat letters, sending small gifts, caring about her former charge. It had been Nanny Hopkins who had taken her in when she'd returned from Italy. Jobless, pregnant and homeless.

And now her dear old friend was gone. Felled by a massive stroke. And this uncaring—uncaring brute—

Tears spilling, she faced him, recent grief making

her chest feel as if it must burst. 'Nothing matters to you unless it comes gold-plated with a breathtaking price tag. Not even other people's feelings!' She heaved back a throat-tearing sob. 'Just get out of my sight! Right out! Just go!'

His face paling beneath the olive tones of his skin, Ettore's eyes narrowed to slits of glittering jet as his proud head came up. No one spoke to him that way. No one!

One searing glance of withering contempt, then, his wallet extracted, he flipped notes onto the floor at her feet. His barely accented voice was terse as he instructed, 'Get your child something more suited to this century.' And he stalked out, washing his hands of the creature for the second time in his life.

CHAPTER TWO

IT WAS no use kidding himself he was listening to Verdi's *Aida*. He had to face up to the irritating fact that almost literally running into Sophie Lang had ruined any hopes of a well-earned relaxing couple of hours before he got down to dealing with the waiting raft of paperwork.

So, hissing impatiently through his strong white teeth, Ettore jettisoned the whole idea and jack-knifed to his feet, abandoning the leather-covered padded lounger and switching off the sound system.

Unsettled, and hating the unprecedented state of affairs—he always knew what he was at, didn't he? Well, didn't he?—he paced over the honey-blonde polished hardwood floor to the sheet of toughened glass that comprised one wall of the penthouse suite's spacious living area. He stared out over city lights shrouded in the misty gloom of late-afternoon, bunching his fists into the pockets of the casual sweats he'd dragged on after he'd showered.

Edgy. Something continually nagging at the back of his mind. Couldn't access it. His ebony brows met in a frown of sheer aggravation. And then he had it.

Guilty conscience!

Which was a bit rich, considering Sophie Lang didn't possess anything remotely like a conscience, he half humorously conceded. But finally pinpointing the source of his edginess made him feel a whole load better—back in control of his head.

He'd been too incensed by the way she'd lashed out at him over the business of that wretched pram to assess the situation calmly. And, come to think of it, her whole attitude during their enforced and regrettable reunion had been confrontational when, from his standpoint, she should have been, if not embarrassed by and apologetic for her past sneak-thief activities, because that was obviously beyond her, then at least suitably and quietly humble.

But for all her lippiness there was no denying she'd been genuinely distressed over the loss of that awful old pram. Sentimental value, as she'd so forcefully told him. If he'd had any inkling of that he wouldn't have offloaded the thing. He'd genuinely thought she would be happy to see the back of the ancient monstrosity and more than grateful to use his cash to buy something more attuned to the needs of a modern mother and her baby.

A mistake, obviously. And an even worse one had been the way he'd tossed that money at her feet with what he now conceded was uncalled-for dismissive arrogance. She'd made him lose his temper, forget the code of manners that had been instilled in him since birth.

That couldn't be remedied, but the other error could. An impatient glance at his gold Rolex showed it was just gone five-thirty. The charity shop might stay open until six. It was worth a try.

Salve his conscience and she'd be out of his head again. No problem. In the aftermath of that dreadful night well over a year ago he'd coldly put her to the back of his mind under the mental heading of Bitter Experience and moved on—right on.

Within seconds he'd shouldered his way into a soft-as-butter black leather jacket, collected his car keys and exited the apartment. The lift carried him smoothly down to the parking area.

He made his destination just as a boot-faced woman was about to lock the shop door. The effortless charm of his smile gained him entry, plus an immediate relaxing of the woman's features into an incongruously girlish simper. The writing of another healthy cheque made out to the charity gained him the promise that the ancient pram would be delivered to the given address first thing in the morning.

Back in the car, waiting his opportunity to ease out into the traffic, Ettore brooded over the ongoing and utterly annoying reality that something was still bugging him.

Still!

But what? Something he didn't want to face?

Ebony brows flared with mounting exasperation. He owed the dishonest little baggage nothing further. Hadn't he picked her up out of the gutter, transported her, her child and her belongings to where she wanted to go? Reclaimed the old pram at inconvenience to himself?

In fact his future wife, the wronged Cinzia di Barsini, would consider his time and energy spent on Sophie Lang's behalf to be way beyond what was necessary or wise. The guy Sophie Lang had moved in with could look out for her. His own conscience was clear. She'd get her precious pram back and that should be the end of the matter.

But it wasn't.

Then the answer to what was still needling at the back of his mind hit him with a force that took his breath away, pumped his heart into overdrive.

Mentally venting a string of curses, he swung the powerful car out into traffic, heading in the direction of Finsbury Circus.

Sophie Lang had one highly pertinent question to answer. And he'd get it if he had to drag it out of her!

'I don't like to dash off and leave you.' Tim Dunmore patted a breast pocket to make sure his wallet was present and correct. 'But Rocko would kill me if I missed his stag night.'

'No worries!' Sophie gave him a warmly affectionate smile. 'You've been really great. I'll never be able to thank you enough for taking us in.'

Her best friend Tina's big brother, whom she hadn't seen for a couple of years, since Tina's wedding to her Canadian boyfriend, had walked into the wine bar where she'd been working one day and had got the whole sorry story from her. She'd been three months pregnant at the time, lodging with Nanny Hopkins, dismissed by the agency and blacklisted for being accused of dishonesty, her protestations of innocence brusquely brushed aside.

Just like Nanny Hopkins, Tim had believed her implicitly, and had written his mobile number on the back of a business card, making her promise to get in touch if she ever needed anything—cash for stuff for the kid when it came, a part-time job at his place of work if he could swing it, a place to crash.

Despite not forseeing any eventuality that would have her asking him for anything, Sophie had kept the card, and when her whole world had crashed around her head she'd been so glad she had.

Nanny Hopkins had seemed as invincible as ever, willingly babysitting Torry while Sophie worked shifts at the local supermarket to support them, so as not to be a drain on the elderly lady's slender resources. Then she had gone. The massive stroke had been so sudden, so shocking.

Grief-stricken, in the middle of making funeral arrangements, she'd been handed the news that as Nanny Hopkins's name had been on the rent book Sophie was to vacate the property in double-quick time. House prices were rocketing. A swift up-grade job and the landlord could sell at a whale of a profit.

Because she'd had Torry to think of she'd swallowed her pride and phoned her stepmother. But the request for somewhere to stay while she got herself sorted had met with a blasé, 'Don't look to me to get you out of a mess of your own making. You should get the kid adopted, for both your sakes. Besides, I'm cultivating a well-heeled widower—no kids of his own, thank heaven—and you and a squawling brat would rather cramp my style. You could try Tiffany, but I don't hold out any hope. She's doing brilliantly, of course, sharing a nice address with two of her model colleagues...'

And on and on, rubbing in her beautiful daughter's breathtaking success on the catwalk against her ordinary stepdaughter's abject failure in every department.

Utterly dispirited, Sophie had cut her stepmother

off in mid-flow. Stacia had never had any time for her. The moment she'd walked in as Sophie's father's new wife she'd dismissed Nanny Hopkins and done all she could to belittle her, pushing her own daughter Tiffany to the fore. Tiffany was so much prettier, so much brighter...

Then she'd remembered Tim's offer of help if she ever needed it.

'I'll always be grateful,' she repeated sincerely now, as Tim grinned down at her.

'No probs! You and Tina were practically joined at the hip when you were kids, so I guess I'm an honorary brother. Anyway, better make tracks.' He headed for the door. 'Don't wait up. Oh, yes.' He turned in the open doorway. 'Tina said she'd call you after she'd had lunch. There's a five-hour time difference, so you should be hearing from her any time now.' And he was gone, leaving Sophie smiling at the space where he had been.

Tim Dunmore was such a dear. Taking her and Torry in, finishing work early so that he could rush back and carry the bulkier of her possessions that the taxi had delivered up the two flights of stairs, finding the bits of the cot and erecting it so that she could put Torry down as soon as he'd been fed...

In fact the Dunmores and Nanny Hopkins had been the nearest thing to a loving family she'd had since her mother had died so tragically young. Tina, her best friend since primary school, had made sure she was invited to spend most of her school holidays with them.

Stacia had been glad to be rid of her, and although she was sure her father must have loved her in his own undemonstrative way, he had been too busy making the money the new wife he was besotted with wanted to spend to show it. He'd worked himself into an early grave trying to keep up with Stacia's demands—which had been like trying to plug a dam with a single piece of straw, because when he'd died he'd been virtually bankrupt.

Swallowing the lump in her throat, she staunchly told herself to forget the past. She could do nothing to change it. The friends she did have were good people, worth their weight in gold, more than making up for the bad. Like Etorre Severini.

But she wasn't going to think about him, was she? Her run-in with him today had been unfortunate, but it didn't mean she had to let him inside her head again—did it?

She had Tina's phone call to look forward to, and as Tina's parents were over there on an extended visit she might get to have a few words with them, too. Thankfully they had all respected her decision to stay silent on the subject of Torry's father. And in the meantime she had the evening paper to look through in her quest for paid employment.

A live-in position as housekeeper to someone who wouldn't object to a child would be ideal. But whoever employed her long-term would ask for references, and the agency that had blacklisted her most certainly wouldn't supply them. The best she could hope for would be something part-time, badly paid and menial. She would never earn enough to pay for proper child care, she thought on a wave of deep despair, and she couldn't sponge off Tim for more than a week or two.

Consciously relegating such unnerving thoughts to the back of her mind, to be taken out and examined later, Sophie checked Torry, peacefully asleep in his blue-painted cot at the side of the narrow bed in Tim's spare room, and had just settled down to scan the Situations Vacant columns when someone knocked on the outer door of the flat. Imperiously.

Someone looking for Tim? Leaving the paper open on the table, she brushed a lock of long blonde hair back from her face and padded barefoot to the door. Immediately she did her best to shut it again, but her strength in no way matched Ettore's as he effortlessly resisted her attempts and walked right in.

Her face flaming with fiery colour, Sophie placed a hand on her breast, where her heart was beating so furiously she couldn't get her breath, her eyes widening painfully as she watched him walk to the centre of the room and then swing abruptly round to face her.

He dominated the space, seeming to charge the very air with electric currents of raw primal energy that touched every nerve-ending, making them fizz. He'd had this effect on her since she'd first set eyes on him. The sexual vibes were intensely shocking. Once the chemistry had overwhelmed her into believing they were meant for each other. She had welcomed it—now she just didn't need it!

'What do you want?' The words came out like the challenge they were, the effect somewhat spoiled by the breathless delivery.

Borderline insolence was the only way to describe the arrogant way he held his unfairly handsome head and the set of those wide shoulders. The soft leather jacket virtually screamed expense and a top-flight designer label, topping what looked like a pair of joggers, and feet encased in a pair of worn trainers.

Only the mega-confident, super-wealthy, with a long line of illustrious ancestors behind them, could get away with that sort of sartorial mix-and-match, was her self-admittedly inconsequential thought as she watched those intelligent eyes narrow to slivers of glittering jet.

Violently ignoring the hateful physical awareness that had never failed to mount a massive full-frontal attack whenever he was near her, she forcefully reminded herself of what a lying, heartless super-snob he really was, and pushed out firmly, 'We have nothing to say to each other.'

The phone rang.

'Answer it.' Ettore's dark head tipped towards the intrusive wall-mounted instrument when Sophie seemed set to ignore it. He watched as mutiny simmered in her clear grey eyes only to give way to sudden compliance as she took the few paces necessary to reach for the receiver.

Watching her, he expelled his breath slowly. He'd been wrong about her being overweight. Narrow-legged well-worn jeans and a shrunken woolly jumper revealed a body that was as delectably voluptuous as he remembered it—the waist tantalisingly tiny in between bountifully luscious breasts and the tempting curves and the feminine flare of her hips.

Lust surged. He didn't want it. He could pick and choose among some of the world's most glamorous women, should he feel inclined—which he didn't—

so why did this devious little baggage make him feel as horny as an adolescent when his sex-drive had been non-existent ever since her true colours had been revealed?

His mouth dried. He swallowed harshly and made himself concentrate on his reason for being here at all. And it had nothing to do with remembering how her warm, seductive flesh had felt beneath his shaping hands before he'd had exactly what she was pushed under his nose.

It had to do with timing, with genes. Her huge eyes were a soft smudgy grey, overlaid with shimmeringly clear crystal, and her long hair was a fascinating silvery blonde. From what he'd seen of the guy she was now shacked up with, he, too, was as blond as they came. So he was highly unlikely to be the father of her baby. And unless she was in the habit of flitting in and out of men's beds...

Only the delayed realisation that the caller was likely to be Tina, and that her friend would only worry needlessly if she didn't pick up, had Sophie obeying an order she'd had every stubborn intention of ignoring.

But it was impossible to carry on an uninhibited conversation under the cold stare of six feet of supremely self-assured intimidating male. And when Tina said, 'You've had a really rotten time of· it. Stacia wouldn't give you the time of day, that goes without saying, but couldn't Torry's father—whoever he is—do something to help?' Sophie pushed in hastily.

'Look, I can't talk right now. I'll phone you back.'

She replaced the receiver and, turning slowly, willed her face to stop glowing like a boiled lobster.

She couldn't have regaled her friend with the information that her baby son was far better off with no father at all rather than one who was a first-class snob, a liar, and a silver-tongued seducer of fanciable members of what he probably regarded as the underclass—not when he was standing like a brooding Nemesis right under her nose, listening to every word she said.

And Ettore Severini must never know that he'd sired a son. Given what she now knew of his character, he'd probably flatly deny any responsibility because—let's face it—he'd already earmarked a classy bride to be the mother of his children. But she couldn't face even the remotest risk that he might want custody of her beautiful baby. Because if he did, he would make damn sure he got it. And where would that leave his child's far from aristocratic, cash-strapped and, in his jaundiced view, sticky-fingered mother?

Nowhere.

'Where are they?' The question emerged with the velocity of a bullet.

Sophie, swallowing sickly, parried, 'Who? What?'

'Your son and your lover.'

'Tim is not my lover,' Sophie stated, tight-lipped. He had no right to question her, but since he looked as if he would stay exactly where he was until he got an answer she preferred to keep his attention on her friend's brother and right away from her baby. 'He's a very good friend and, not that it's any of your business, he is out for the evening.'

'Right.' An ebony brow was slightly elevated in a gesture intended to convey that he wasn't buying the just-good-friends bit. Not that she cared one way or the other. His opinion of her was rock bottom, so it couldn't go any lower.

Shaking inside, her legs feeling like chewed string, she walked to the door and held it open. 'Please leave. You must have had a reason for coming here, but whatever it is I'm not interested.'

Being with him again brought too many memories back, most of them so beautiful they were full of pain because they were founded on cynically expert seduction techniques. He'd shown himself for exactly what he was on that last evening. And she didn't want to remember that, either.

'No?'

Sophie whitened. She didn't know how a simple two-letter word could sound like the direst threat. But it did. Her stomach jumped.

Horribly aware of those narrowed jet eyes on her, she quivered. The soles of her bare feet were cringing on the strip of cold lino, and a howling draught was gusting up the stairs like a force ten gale, but she stood her ground, willing him to leave.

He didn't. He simply strode over and closed the door decisively behind her, then asked with a smooth urbanity that chilled her to the bone, 'So, exactly how old is he?'

A hot surge of adrenalin made her want to run like the wind, set her heart knocking against her ribs. She'd been absolutely dreading this ever since he'd found her in the gutter. Had been hoping and praying that the ultra-wealthy, sophisticated, smooth-as-oil banker would have about as much interest in a small baby as he would in a passing ant.

Still clinging to that very slight hope, she lifted her chin and snipped out, 'Twenty-eight.'

Madre di Dio! She was pushing her luck here! Ettore held onto his speedily dwindling patience and pointed out, 'I'm not remotely interested in learning anything about the man you've just moved in with. How old is your baby?'

Sophie felt her already shaky knees weaken even further. The bitten-out question was a glaring signpost to the way his mind was working. She clamped her teeth together, tightening her lips, saying nothing.

Ettore, the calculations he'd already made at the forefront of his mind, queried smoothly, 'Seven months?'

Sophie's heart felt like a cold, heavy stone. This was turning into a nightmare. Her mouth ran dry as she lifted her eyes to his, trying to formulate something telling that would leave him in no doubt that she and her baby were off-limits as far as he and his delving questions were concerned.

But Ettore got in first, his voice as chilling as the dark glint in his eyes. 'You told me you were protected and I took you at your word. I may have been as misguided in that as in everything else. Reckless must be your middle name.'

Hatefully, and predictably, Sophie felt her face flame. He already believed she was reckless enough to steal a highly valuable piece of jewellery from under his fiancée's nose. But reckless enough to have unprotected sex and lie about it?

She had been taking the contraceptive pill, but

sometimes—probably owing to what had happened on the island, the world-toppling event of finding the love of her life and believing that he felt exactly the same, caring for the twins—sometimes she'd plain forgotten.

And the fiery state of her face would be telling him more than she wanted him to know.

Dark eyes glittering, his spectacular bone structure hardening, he spelt out, 'You may have been enjoying the rampant sex I know you're so hooked on with some guy before I arrived at the villa. My brother-in-law's gardener also has dark eyes and hair. It's certainly a consideration. But perhaps you can enlighten me? Or don't you know who the father is?'

His jaw tightened forcefully and Sophie paled at the insulting opinion of her morals. She couldn't have spoken a word if her life had depended on it, and felt mortally sick.

'You are obviously not going to enlighten me,' he asserted coldly. And then, astonishing her, turned on his heels and paced towards the door.

He was leaving! He had no further interest in Torry—in whether the baby was his or someone else's! A dry sob of relief swelled in her chest. Her fear that he might guess Torry was his son and insist that custody was rightfully his, take her baby from her to be brought up in the style that befitted his father's illustrious bloodlines, had been unfounded and foolish.

But no sooner had the relief allowed her to uncurl her tightly fisted fingers than her misconception was dealt a savage blow.

Ettore Severini turned one last time, the door already partly open. 'I mean to have the truth. I suggest you sleep on it. If, tomorrow, you still refuse to answer then I will find all the evidence I need. A simple DNA test will do it.'

Halfway down the dreary flight of stairs Ettore was already speaking on his mobile. In the past the bank had had occasion to use the services of a discreet and highly efficient firm of private investigators. Reaching his car, he ended the call. Someone would be here within minutes. Someone would watch. And if she tried to do a runner with her child—his child?—she would be followed and her whereabouts dutifully reported.

His eyes narrowed with lethal anger as he slid behind the steering wheel. If the dark-eyed, dark-haired child was his, and the increasing tug of gut instinct told him he was, then she would discover that there was nowhere to hide.

CHAPTER THREE

NO YOUNG lady, with or without a babe in arms, had been observed leaving the premises. That was the information Ettore received as he strode through the crisp morning towards Finsbury Circus, preferring to use up a fraction of his restless energy rather than sit behind the wheel of his hired car as it crept through the appalling rush hour traffic.

As Sophie Lang's present address came into view Ettore ended his call, together with the agent's assignment, and the unremarkable car parked on the opposite side of the street pulled discreetly away. He slotted the mobile into an inside pocket of his suit jacket, uninterested in the further signing off information that a tall fair-haired young man had taken delivery of a big black pram as he'd been hurrying out of the premises at just before nine this morning, taking off at speed a few moments later.

That her latest lover had already left for work, running late, by the sound of it—because of a night of steamy sex with Sophie?—was neither here nor there, and the hard hot knot that twisted in his gut was not down to jealousy. Of course not. Most definitely not. Just completely understandable anger that his maybe-baby faced a childhood under the doubtful care of a numberless succession of 'uncles' and a mother with no morals worth mentioning.

If the child was his.

And swift as a knife the astounding thought that he wanted the child to be his slashed into his mind, rooting his feet into the pavement for shell-shocked seconds. Until the momentary aberration passed and he was able to haul himself smartly together, grit his teeth and mount the steps with his honed jaw at a determined angle.

One way or another, he was going to find out.

Have a nice nap, my own precious darling,' Sophie breathed as she laid the sleepy infant down in his cot, gently tucking the soft-as-down covers around him as the thick lashes that framed his huge brown eyes finally drifted closed.

Quietly leaving the tiny bedroom, she stood still for a moment, drawing in a deep breath, still miraculously holding herself together. Just about.

Torry's bellows for his breakfast had broken into her restless dreams at just before five-thirty. So the entirely pleasurable business of feeding him, bathtime, and the gentle playtime that was always so special had kept the demons at bay.

Now they were marching back, all teeth and claws, terrifying her!

She was going to have to tell Ettore Severini, she acknowledged with a lurch of her stomach, confess that Torry was his son. Apart from packing their bags and taking off—destination unknown—she couldn't see a way out of it.

He was already deeply suspicious, and if she tried to lie about it he would insist on having that DNA test and get to the truth. And that would hand him further evidence of what he saw as her deceitful character—another nasty label to pin on her. Yet another label he could use should he—heaven help her!—decide to go for custody.

So she would have to tell him and hope to goodness he would see sense, see that publicly acknowledging his son would do his relationship with his wife no good at all. From what she remembered of his then fiancée's cold black eyes, her beautiful but frigid features, she didn't have a forgiving bone in her body.

She felt physically sick. Remembering. She didn't want to remember, and pressed cold fingertips to her burning temples to try to block it all out again. But it didn't work, and the scenes that had led to what happened on that last dreadful night replayed remorselessly through her cringing mind like an endlessly recurring nightmare.

She and the four-year-old Valenti twins, Matteo and Amalia, had returned from the island the day before—Ettore having left the day before that, to attend what he had announced was an unexpected and urgent business meeting. On the mainland Signor Valenti had met the private launch—to the delight of his children, who hadn't seen Mama or Papa for four whole weeks.

As the company helicopter had taken off for Florence Signor Valenti had sighed. 'Such a summer! No escape this year for my wife and I from the heat of the city—too many pressing business meetings and entertainings. Poor Flavia complains of being wilted, and she is pining to see her children again. She would be here with us now, but she is deep in the arrangements for her birthday party.'

Sophie did her best to look really sympathetic, but she knew she wasn't. If the Valentis hadn't had to do without their annual escape to their villa on the island then Ettore, Flavia's brother, wouldn't have been pressed into dropping by to make sure the temporary nanny was coping.

And they wouldn't have found each other, fallen passionately in love, made each other so blissfully happy. And now the island idyll was over, and in a day or two she'd be returning to England—because the children's permanent nanny was fully recovered and waiting for her charges in the elegant house in the Oltrano district on the other side of the Arno where, traditionally, the prosperous ruling families resided.

But it wasn't really over—not by a long chalk! Ettore hadn't proposed, not in so many words, but every tingling instinct told her that he knew they were meant to be together for all time. Hadn't he, on his last night on the island, promised to escort her back to London, hinting that they had much to discuss?

Back in Florence, on Sophie's final day, Flavia warmly pressed her to join the lavish birthday celebrations planned for that evening. Already the overnighting guests had started to arrive—prominent among them the spectacularly glamorous Cinzia di Barsini, travelling with her obsequious, mousy personal maid.

'You are no longer employed as a nanny—until you leave us in the morning you are our valued guest. Please don't disappoint me!'

Faced with such a warm invitation from her

charming erstwhile employer, Sophie could only agree, though her natural inclination would have led her to keep well out of the way rather than spend the evening among a crowd of ultra-sophisticated strangers.

And only the absolute conviction that Ettore would be attending his sister's birthday celebrations had her scrabbling through the suitcase she'd just packed, ready for her early-morning departure, looking for something vaguely suitable to wear.

She hadn't seen him since he'd left the island, but she wouldn't let herself get uptight about that. He was a busy man. But a man of his word. She trusted him without reservation. So he'd be here this evening, if not earlier, and he'd been adamant about returning to London with her, making plans for their future.

The party was in full swing when Sophie ventured to join it. Still no sign of Ettore. She was doing her level best not to be anxious at his continued non-appearance.

The large salon, with its tall, elegantly proportioned windows, walls of soft dusky rose, immense gilt-framed mirrors and glittering chandeliers was alive with the buzz of the great and the good at play. The women in their designer gowns, jewels in their beautifully styled hair, made her feel as out of place as a big sticky bun on a dish of hand-made Belgian chocolates.

She'd thought the light cream-coloured cotton dress with its full knee-length skirt and fitted bodice would pass muster. But it didn't. It was hopelessly old-fashioned and bargain basement, and she would have crept back to her room if Flavia hadn't taken her arm and insisted on introducing her to the nearest knot of guests, taking a glass of champagne from one of the smoothly circulating waiters and pressing it into her hand.

It was on the tip of her tongue to come straight out with it and ask her hostess if Ettore was expected when she saw him.

In the arched doorway. Talking to the glamorous Cinzia di Barsini. Her heart swooped and soared on a rollercoaster of relief, and she hated herself for allowing, even for the smallest moment, those utterly unworthy anxieties to creep in. How could she have allowed herself to wonder if he wasn't going to show up before her flight in the morning, if he had no intention of seeing her again? He loved her, and what they'd shared had been special for both of them—it hadn't been a brief holiday fling!

Love melted her bones, made her clear grey eyes limpid. He was so indescribably beautiful. He wore his cream dinner jacket and narrow dark trousers with elegant urbanity and, unsmiling, the perfection of his features took her breath away. And he was hers! Unbelievable, but wonderfully, gloriously true!

Moving slightly away from the group she was with, she willed him to look up and see her. And as if she'd shouted the command at pitched volume his stunning eyes lifted from the coldly beautiful features of the woman who was engaging him in seemingly deadly serious conversation, found hers and held for a moment, cranking up the already fluttery feeling in the base of her tummy and setting her heart racing, exactly replicating the sensations that had turned her near-naked body to quivering jelly when he'd appeared in the isolated cove on that warm, starlit Italian evening just as she'd been emerging from the gentle swell of the water.

Then his attention was recaptured by something Cinzia said, by the tender, slightly tremulous smile she gave him, the touch of her long white fingers on the sleeve of his jacket.

Sophie sipped her champagne, stupefyingly happy. He would join her when that woman had stopped bending his ear. He was far too well-mannered to brush her aside.

As Flavia performed that task for him, swooping across the floor to place both hands on her brother's shoulders and stand on tiptoe to flutter kisses, continental-fashion, Sophie's lush lips curved in a gooey smile as her beloved Ettore extracted a long, slim jeweller's box from an inner breast pocket and put it in his sister's hands. His birthday gift.

She was contentedly watching the happy tableau, mooning over him, because mooning with a besotted grin on her face felt as natural as breathing, when Cinzia di Barsini slid up to her with the sinuous silence of a snake. The analogy was heightened by the black sequinned gown that clung everywhere it touched, and that was everywhere, and the cold black eyes glittering with venom.

A huff of breath disguised the emergence of a giggle at her own fanciful notions, but all thoughts of giggling or smiling ever again fled when Cinzia drawled patronisingly, 'Might I make a suggestion? Make yourself scarce. Seeing the hired help gawping at my fiancé only causes embarrassment for everyone concerned. You've got the hots for him and it is so uncool. I know he spent three weeks on the island with you and the twins—purely in a supervisory capacity, dear Flavia being naturally unsure of your capabilities.'

A slight understanding lift of the elegant shoulders accompanied the statement. 'And, knowing him, Ettore probably flirted a little to relieve the tedium. It is in the nature of the Italian male to do so. It would mean absolutely nothing. So do us all a favour, especially Ettore, and forget it—whatever 'it' is. He has already said he almost gave the party a miss because he knew you'd be hanging around him like a lovesick calf, just as you did on the island, boring the socks off him, but he knew he and I had some serious work to put in on the last-minute plans for our upcoming wedding.'

As the Italian woman had glided away Sophie had felt physically sick. She could still remember the feeling—remember how she'd shuddered with cold and nausea as Cinzia had rejoined Flavia, who had been admiring the emerald-studded bracelet her brother had fastened round her wrist, touching Ettore's arm, saying something. Something urgent, judging by the look on her face, and the swift frown that had momentarily darkened his fantastic face.

Turning, they had left the room together, and Sophie had sunk onto a small gilded chair because her shaking legs had given up on her. So he wasn't even going to speak to her. He'd be too busy being up close and private with his bride-to-be, discussing wedding plans. She had hardly been able to take it in.

Had all that passion been false, everything he'd said a lie? His seduction merely an exercise in boredom relief? It had truly been almost impossible to believe. And yet the Barsini woman wouldn't have claimed to be his fiancée, on the point of celebrating their marriage, if it weren't the truth. What would she gain by telling lies that could so easily be disproved?

People had begun to look at her. An unfashionably plump creature in a cheap dress, perched on a gilded chair and looking as if her world had fallen apart.

Which it had.

Summoning all her will-power, she'd got to her feet and walked over to where Flavia was still turning her wrist this way and that, admiring her brother's gift. She'd had to make sure. Cinzia might have been lying. She hadn't been able to imagine why, but stranger things had happened.

'It's so lovely,' she'd said, her voice sounding thin in her ears, meaning the bracelet.

'*Si*. Ettore has always spoiled me!' Flavia gave her lovely smile, and Sophie took her courage in both hands and did her best to look relaxed as she replied.

'Then he's bound to spoil Cinzia, too. I hear they're betrothed.' Privately she'd thought the verb sounded really old-fashioned, but she had been unable to say the words 'engaged to be married' because they would have choked her. She tacked on as a breathy afterthought, 'She is very beautiful.'

Flavia's smile faded. 'Beauty is only skin deep. However, many advantages will come from a union which was our late father's dearest wish.' Then she brightened, 'Come, shall we mingle? I will introduce you to—'

'I'm sorry…' Sophie pushed out on a whisper. Stupid to have pinned her hopes on Flavia flatly denying the engagement. There was a strange roaring sound in her ears and the floor seemed to shift beneath her feet. 'You'll have to excuse me. Migraine.'

'Oh, my dear!' Flavia was full of concern. 'What can I do? Shall I call the housekeeper? You are very pale! Do you have something you can take?'

'I just need to lie down. Please don't worry.' She felt such a fraud, but a migraine was the only excuse she could think of to save her the agony of trying to talk to people and pretend she wasn't howling and screaming inside. 'By morning I'll be fine,' she promised, trying to look as if she meant it, knowing it would be a long time before she felt anything like fine again.

And with a final wobbly smile she made it from the crowded room, noting the Barsini woman's personal maid creeping down the stairs in the deserted great hall, wearing an odd look of triumph on her narrow, sallow face.

Ignoring the other woman's simpering, *'Buona sera, signorina,'* because she couldn't trust herself to speak to anyone without bursting into floods of tears, Sophie headed for a distant side door that led to the rear courtyard garden, found a stone bench and sat there, letting the warm scented darkness wrap itself around her.

She had some serious thinking to do, plus a whole lot of growing up.

How pathetically green she'd been to believe a

word he'd said! He was a highly sophisticated creature, scion of a world-respected banking family, fabulously wealthy, charismatic, and stunning to look
at. Why would he consider tying himself to a nobody
who had only one thing going for her—a shaming
willingness to jump into bed with him?

The truth made her cringe and hurt like hell, but
she'd just have to take it, wouldn't she? She could
run Ettore to earth, spill out her pain and anger, but
that would only make her look even more of a gul-
lible fool. She wasn't the first woman to be swept
off her feet and into the bed of an unprincipled
charmer, and she wouldn't be the last.

How long she sat there, with the moonlight touching a statue of Pan, making it glimmer palely through
the surrounding dark foliage, she would never know.
All she did know, as she used the service stairs to
silently creep up to her room in the nursery quarters,
was that she might have lost her heart but she still
had her dignity.

And if—and it was a big if—Ettore did seek her
out before her departure she would rise to the occasion. No tears or passionate recriminations. Just a
throwaway comment that, provided he let her know
the date of his wedding, she would send them a nice
little toaster. With ribbons on.

But he wouldn't seek her out, she acknowledged
as she got ready for bed. It was late now, and although no sounds from the main reception areas
could penetrate into the peaceful atmosphere of the
nursery rooms she guessed the party would be over.
And Ettore, the pressing last-minute plans for his
forthcoming wedding having been sorted out with his

future wife, would have scarpered—no room in his head for the no-account temporary member of staff he'd amused himself with as an antidote to the tedium of being stuck on the family's small private island, where the pace of life was slower than the crawl of a geriatric snail.

She had to accept it, acknowledge that she'd been used by a master charmer, try to put the pain of it behind her and somehow get on with the rest of her life.

Gulping down a sob, she opened her case and stuffed the cream dress in any old how.

She would never see him again. Loving him had become her whole world, and in spite of what she'd been told this evening she couldn't just turn it off. She turned to the bed, hating the knowledge that she was going to spend the night crying her eyes out, and then gasped with alarm as the door to her bedroom was flung open.

Silence—just the dying echo of her own shocked gasp for air. And Cinzia di Barsini, framed in the doorway, the sequins that spangled on her black gown glinting as cruelly as her coal-dark eyes. Then, from behind her, Ettore shouldered into the room. His jacket had been discarded and his cream silk shirt was open at the neck, revealing the oiled satin of his bronzed skin—the skin that had been her delight.

But his face was pale, the fabulous bone structure clenched tight beneath the skin, and his eyes were bleak. The sensual mouth that was capable of giving mind-shattering ecstasy was drawn into a tight line as his beautiful, aristocratic fiancée swept an imperious hand towards Sophie's battered suitcase.

'Open it! It will be there. If not, then search every inch of this room.'

'What do you think you're doing?' At a huge disadvantage in one of the ancient T-shirts she usually wore to bed, her sun-streaked blonde hair all over the place, Sophie knew her question had emerged sounding like the bleating of a frightened child rather than the voice of a justifiably outraged adult.

Cinzia ignored her, advancing on the suitcase and prodding it with the pointy toe of an expensive shoe, and Ettore said tightly, 'Accusations have been made.'

Half turning, he beckoned, and Cinzia's personal maid sidled in, her eyes shifty. Sophie's stomach lurched. She had no idea what was going on, but whatever it was she didn't like it.

Her eyes full of bewildered appeal, she demanded unsteadily, 'What accusations, Ettore?'

'That you have stolen from me!' Cinzia said with utter contempt. 'Filomena, repeat what you saw, so there can be no mistake.'

The staccato burst of Italian was impossible to follow. Sophie could only understand if the delivery was clear and relatively slow. Besides, how could she concentrate when her head was spinning with the shaming accusation? She gave a whimper of distress, tightly banded pain wrapping around her chest as, probably to set the record straight, Ettore translated heavily.

'Filomena claims to have seen you coming from Cinzia's room a couple of hours ago. When she asked, thinking you'd been looking for her mistress, you refused to give an answer.'

'I haven't been near her room,' Sophie denied hotly. 'I don't even know which one she's using!' Her legs threatened to give way beneath her. 'I haven't stolen anything!'

Ettore carried on tautly, as if her outburst hadn't happened, 'Cinzia had left her jewel case open on her dressing table. On retiring she discovered that a highly valuable item was missing.' He glanced at the woman she had learned he was to marry as if for confirmation. 'A diamond choker?' Receiving Cinzia's tight-lipped nod of assent, he sighed heavily and intoned, 'She rang for Filomena, to ask if she moved it, and was told how you'd been seen leaving the room while everyone was occupied at the party.'

'I haven't taken anything!' Sophie wailed, at her wits' end, humiliation piling on humiliation with alarming speed. 'How could you believe I have?' she demanded.

How could he? Even though he'd deceived her, used her, surely after those long nights of shared passion, when he'd made her believe that heaven itself could hold no greater happiness, after the laughter they'd shared as they'd played with the children, the lazy picnics, the late-night intimate suppers for two, he had grown to know her well enough to know she was at least honest?

The frown line between his eyes increased as, taking matters into her own hands, Filomena bent down to open the suitcase. Sophie surged forward to stop the invasion of her privacy. Ettore's hand stayed her.

The touch of his strong, beautifully crafted fingers on the bare flesh of her arm filled her throat with raw emotion, and she was sure compassion lurked at the back of his fine eyes as he murmured thickly, 'I apologise for this. There is nothing to fear. I promise.'

But there was. Sophie knew it in her bones. Bones that were shaking, unfortunately adding to the impression of guilt. She'd been set up. By the maid? By Cinzia herself? It seemed totally ridiculous, but she knew it was a fact when Filomena gave a screech of triumph and jerked to her feet, her outstretched hand displaying the jewel.

After that, she was too deep in shock to say another word in her own defence, not even when Ettore asked harshly, 'Well?'

Her eyes wide in the pallor of her face, her mouth quivering uncontrollably, Sophie fought against the hot tide of rising nausea. Her eyes were a mute appeal for time to pull herself together, get her head around this latest horror.

She knew he was believing the evidence of his own eyes, and this coming on top of learning he was about to be married, had taken her love and tossed it aside as if it had no more value than a used bus ticket, was the final incapacitating blow to a brain that was already too traumatised to function.

'So. Nothing to say.' Ettore gave her one long, unreadable look, turned on his heels and walked out, his head high, his shoulders rigid.

His future wife had taken the key from the inside of the door. 'I will make sure you are released when the driver arrives to take you to the airport in the morning. Be thankful that I'm not in the mood for pressing charges. It would give me pleasure to know you were behind bars, but I have my wedding to think of, and that is all the pleasure I need at this moment.'

Sophie swallowed the lump in her throat, wondering wildly if, after all, she and Torry should make a run for it. Find somewhere to hide out until he shrugged those impressive shoulders, gave up looking for them, and returned to Italy. And his wife.

The resurgence, in such vivid and painful detail, of the memories she'd shoved to the back of her mind was making her lose all sense of proportion, she decided, and made herself summon all that remained of her common sense. Running out into the street with nowhere to go would be the worst thing she could do for her baby.

She had to tough it out, she assured herself as she went to the window overlooking the street, hoping against hope that he'd changed his mind and wouldn't bother to show up. What would a wealthy Italian banker and his aristocratic wife want with his bastard son? Or the adverse publicity of a custody battle?

Torry was her much loved child. Surely he would see it would be a crime to separate him from his mother.

But he would say she wasn't fit to rear his child to manhood. And all the reasons he could summon up to back that premise made her feel decidedly queasy. Her insides jumping with nerves, she changed her mind and wished he'd arrive so they could get the threatened interview over. Only then could she begin to try to find a solution to her present unenviable homeless and near penniless situation.

And then she saw him, approaching the street door with an intimidating, purposeful stride. Her heart lurched, and on impulse she opened the flat door and shot down the stairs to meet him. She knew she was being irrational in wanting to keep him at as much distance as possible from her innocently sleeping son, and in her haste to reach the door, to keep him on the steps before he could enter, she collided with a large solid object and went sprawling on the floor.

Deploring the complete lack of security attached to the house, Ettore mounted the steps and swung open the front door. Biting back a caustic comment at the sight of the mother of his maybe-child sitting on the dusty floor for no sensible reason he could fathom, he swept his eyes over her pink-flushed features, the tangle of long silky blonde hair, noting the way her wide eyes swept incredulously between him and the dreadful old pram.

He extended a hand, determinedly hardening his heart, scorning the way its tendency to turn mushy at her surely manufactured air of vulnerability.

Ignoring that seemingly imperious hand gesture, Sophie scrambled to her feet. She didn't need his help.

But she couldn't help wondering, even softening. 'You got my pram back for me?'

He dipped his dark head in terse agreement. How well he remembered that look—all wide-eyed innocence, clear and direct, with the underlying sparkle of warmth and wonderment. All the act of a seasoned con-artist. It was the reminder he needed.

'Not personally,' he disclaimed coolly, disregarding his last-minute dash to the charity shop, the shelling out of a further hefty donation. 'I wouldn't be seen dead pushing that heap of old iron through the streets. But you appeared to be unaccountably attached to the thing. I merely arranged to have it returned to you.'

Sophie stared at him, wide-eyed. He had done her a real kindness. It might have been in tune with the man she'd fallen head over heels in love with, but it didn't gel with the man he had eventually shown himself to be. Shamelessly cheating on his fiancée, seducing and deceiving the hired help, hinting at happy-ever-after and all that stuff, then believing anyone's word over hers and branding her a thief. Not forgetting the way he'd contacted the agency and made sure she never worked on her chosen career path again.

But… 'Thank you,' she uttered sincerely. That much at least was due to him, though his mean, moody and arrogant stance told her he didn't rate the concession.

Cold eyes pinned her to the spot, and Sophie shivered in the arctic blast, wrapping her arms around her body to hold herself together.

Crunch time.

She knew it.

Even prepared for it, she still felt a tide of nausea rise within her as he stated chillingly, 'You have something to tell me.'

CHAPTER FOUR

SOPHIE was only too aware that she had to be giving an award-winning impression of a fish out of water as the words that could seal Torry's fate hovered on the tip of her tongue—only to be convulsively swallowed back again. And, equally demoralising, she felt her knees weaken treacherously beneath her, felt what colour she did have leach out of her skin beneath the hard challenge of those glittering dark eyes.

He looked as cold and unapproachable as the far side of the moon, and the prospect of actually saying the words that would give him rights over her precious baby was scaring her silly. She lowered her own eyes to the floor and gave a huge shudder of reaction when his tension-riven voice arrowed at her downbent head.

'Upstairs. We can't talk in this benighted hole.'

That restored the loss of her vocal chords quicker than any surgical procedure. 'Of course we can,' she yelped, panic stricken. 'It won't take more than two seconds flat!'

She didn't want him anywhere near her baby. He might demand to take a good long look at the fruit of his loins. And no one seeing the little charmer could fail to fall in love with him. Not even a hard-hearted brute like Ettore Severini.

Not giving him the chance to argue the toss, she made herself spit it out, not letting herself wimp out.

'Torry is your son. But, listen, I promise to make no demands of any kind on you. No one but I—and now you—knows who his father is, and never will. Your wife need never know—there's no reason for her to be upset. You can forget about both of us.'

'Where is he? In the flat?'

Taking in the feverish glitter of those dark eyes, the faint flush of colour now washing the fascinating arch of his prominent cheekbones, Sophie knew he hadn't taken in a word she'd said beyond the stunning fact that he was a father. And where else would he think her baby was? Put out with the garbage? What kind of mother did he think she was?

No, don't answer that, she informed her whirling brain as anxiety formed an acid ball in her tummy, increasing a thousandfold when he brushed past her, heading for the stairs, taking them two at a time.

Her throat convulsing, Sophie gathered her shocked wits and sped after him, her eyes transfixed by the rigid determination of his broad back. His actions weren't those of a man who would shrug his shoulders and walk away, dismissing the existence of an illegitimate son—even though he'd just been handed the opportunity to do so on a plate.

But then he hadn't taken in her statement that she'd make no demands on him, that the identity of Torry's father would remain their secret, she hastily rationalised as he pushed the door to Tim's flat fully open and walked on through.

A frantic spurt of activity brought her to his side as he reached the centre of the unprepossessing living area. Her instinctive restraining hand on his arm had him dealing her a clenched brow look that was as savage as a physical assault. Sophie tried not to flinch and struggled to get her breath back as he shrugged her hand aside. But he was a reasonable man, surely? Once she'd grabbed his full attention and reinforced her earlier statement—no demands, a secret kept—he'd—

'So where is he?' He denied her the opportunity to say anything, striding to the inner door that led to the two tiny bedrooms.

He was impossible! Big, domineering—something else! Perhaps he'd listen to her when he'd sated his curiosity. That was her self-admitted feeble thought as she resigned herself to leading the way to the box-like room Tim had allowed her to use.

Opening the door with deliberate care, because she'd discovered the hinges protested gratingly if not treated with the utmost respect, Sophie stood aside and allowed Ettore to enter, her breath snagging in her throat and her heart beating as if it had gone crazy.

Would one look at his sleeping son satisfy him? Alarmingly, she didn't think so. He was not easily satisfied, was he? Her face reddened as she shamingly recalled how insatiable he'd been on the island—insatiable for sex, she reminded herself hollowly, not for her as a loved individual, just for sex with the nearest halfway presentable willing woman.

One look at his son would never be enough, instinct now told her. And the look was long, lingering—as if he was absorbing every detail of the tiny features, the soft sleep-flushed skin and the mop of silky black hair.

At last he turned, and the tenderness tinged with

something that looked suspiciously like pride she was sure she had fleetingly glimpsed was replaced by tough aggression as he told her, 'We need to talk.'

'Of course.' Her spine rigid, Sophie led the way back to the living area. 'And maybe this time you'll listen.'

She refused to be intimidated by his anger, refused to sit when he gestured towards the leather-covered three-seater.

'As I said—'

'I know what you said.' He brusquely cut her off. 'No demands. Secrets. Do you imagine for one fluff-brained moment that I would be ashamed to acknowledge my own son? Blood of my blood! That I would wash my hands of him and leave him to be brought up fatherless, relying on his mother's latest lover for a roof of sorts over his head, the bread in his mouth?' His own mouth was hard with bitter condemnation. 'Dragged up with no real security, with no moral principles to guide him!'

'How dare you say that?' Sophie shot at him with fierce outrage. Her fisted hands knuckled firmly on her curvy hips. 'Hypocrite! How many moral principles did you have when you seduced me, vowed you loved me, and all the time you were engaged to marry someone else?'

Huge grey eyes sparked with an angry flare of triumph as she noted his immediate discomfiture, the way the long dark sweep of his lashes lowered to hide his expressive eyes. A muscle jerked at the side of his hard, blue-black shadowed jaw, and Sophie suddenly felt compassion swell like a big soft ball inside her heart.

She didn't know why, but she really hated to see him at a disadvantage—even though she knew he deserved everything she'd thrown at him. Had she thrown enough to get him off her case? The possibility should be filling her with elation, but all she felt was a weird emptiness.

Ettore Severini was not a man to be routed so easily, and his slightly accented voice was cool and smooth as he commented, 'It is pointless to rake over past sins when we need to concentrate on the present and the future of our son.'

He saw the lush pout of her mouth quiver, then tighten, and his heart gave a savage jerk as he remembered how that mouth had felt beneath his, how incredibly responsive she'd been. He'd been blown away.

Agreeing to his sister's plea that he drop in on the family's secluded holiday home—'Just for forty-eight hours to check that Sophie's coping. I'm sure she is. During the weeks she's been with us she's been perfect in every respect. Call me clucky if you like, but it would set my mind at rest.'

In the event forty-eight hours had stretched to three weeks.

Arriving on the island that first evening, he'd been deeply troubled. The future of his personal life had suddenly seemed so achingly empty.

The long-standing arrangement he had with Cinzia di Barsini, only child of his father's friend and one-time business colleague, negotiated primarily by both sets of parents, had always seemed acceptable—entirely normal.

In the elevated circles he moved in marriage was

regarded as a merger, with family name, social standing and wealth the accepted currency. Marrying for the ephemeral emotion named love was for lesser beings—people who did not carry the responsibility of huge estates, business and banking empires on their shoulders.

Consolidating wealth and status was a set-in-concrete duty that must be followed. That was the tenet that had been drummed into him almost from birth. And sensibly accepted.

But recently something inside him had started to rebel, to question. Could there be something more than the empty union that lay somewhere in his future?

Cinzia had always been honest, a trusted friend. 'We're not madly in love with each other—but that sort of romantic candyfloss is for airheads. We value and respect each other, and that, for intelligent adults, has to be a more lasting basis for a meaningful relationship. We will marry when you decide you want an heir. And I will give you heirs,' she had told him, when the death of his father had had her family pressing for their marriage.

Her smooth cool hand had briefly touched his, her smile—as it always was for him—had been pure sweetness and light. 'Unlike Papa, I understand that your loss means a mountain of more work for you. We can wait a little while longer. I'm in no hurry to settle down, and as your future bride I will remain untouched—that goes without saying.' She had primmed her mouth fastidiously. 'If you have certain needs, in the meantime, I do insist the way you satisfy them is not brought to my attention.'

At the time he hadn't seen the lack of what people called love as a problem. In the upper stratum of society such an arrangement was entirely acceptable. Dynastic marriages worked well far more often than not. And no eyebrows were raised when a man took a mistress. Besides, his life was full, intensely satisfying. Work filled most of his waking hours, and the women who filled the remaining corners—though not as many as he'd been credited with—knew the score.

When he finally said goodbye to his bachelor freedom he would gain a beautiful, wealthy, ultra-sophisticated wife to give him an heir and run his household elegantly, to act as a brilliant hostess. Could any man ask for more?

But in the weeks preceding his agreement to check on Flavia's children and the temporary nanny doubts had tormented him—until he'd reached a decision to break his engagement. There had to be more than such emptiness, such shallowness.

His father would turn in his grave, and his mother, now permanently living with a paid companion in a lavish Venice apartment, would disapprove. But he couldn't live his life the way they wanted him to, hidebound by rules that he now saw as positively medieval. For the first time in his life he wanted to find what poets called love—if it existed. And as Cinzia's emotions had never been engaged the di Barsini family would look around for another suitable merger. No one would suffer from his decision.

He would tell her of his decision to break the engagement when he returned to Florence. In person. Giving her the option of letting it be known that it was she who'd had second thoughts and called it off, saving the pride that was so important to her.

It was at that point in his deliberations that he had announced his arrival to the resident cook/housekeeper, had checked on his sleeping niece and nephew and, still edgy, wandered down to the moonlit cove—to be struck by a shaft of primeval lust such as he'd never experienced before.

He'd watched the temporary nanny slowly emerge from the glassy water, moonlight silvering her luscious body, clad in the tiniest triangles of fabric, her arms above and behind her head, thrusting her ripe breasts into tempting prominence as she rung seawater from her long blonde hair.

And in the days that had followed, as he'd grown to know her—or thought he had, he now amended—lust had rapidly blossomed into love. Such love as he'd never expected to experience or even believed possible.

Everything about her had delighted and fascinated him. She was like no other woman he had ever met in his social or business circles. She was warm and funny, generous with the unforced love she lavished on Flavia's children, and completely natural, with no hint of the artifice that seemed the stock in trade of most of the women he came into contact with.

She didn't flirt, he doubted that she would know how, but reciprocal desire had simmered in the depths of her huge smoky-grey eyes, and he had been stingingly aware of her heightened flush, the rush of her indrawn breath if they happened to touch.

Making love had been so natural, so right. It had had the inevitability of night following day. And her generosity, her willing response, had blown his mind, enslaved him utterly.

She hadn't been a virgin. He'd accepted that. This was the twenty-first century, after all. As an Italian male he would have preferred to be the first with this woman he'd already decided he could never be parted from, but he'd prided himself on being pretty laid-back about it. And he'd believed her when, after that magical first time, she'd confided that she had never believed it could be like that. So wonderful, so earth-shattering.

Looking at her now—all silky blonde hair, limpid eyes, kissable lips and soft womanly curves—a surge of anger so savage it threatened to send him into orbit brought a red mist in front of his eyes. He dragged a long breath through pinched nostrils as he controlled it. It wasn't directed at her, not primarily, but at himself—for acting like a lovestruck loon, allowing her to pull the wool so thoroughly over his eyes, blinding him to what she really was.

A promiscuous thief.

Barely sparing her a further glance—in his present mood he couldn't bear to look at her—he pointed out, 'I had hoped never to have to see you again, but, that being said, we have to put the past behind us and concentrate on our son. Please sit.'

Flooded with self-loathing for ever believing this monster was the best human being ever to draw breath, for naively believing that such a sophisticated, filthy rich hunk could have any long-term interest in an ordinary nobody like her, Sophie capitulated with bad grace and sat down stiffly onto one end of the long leather sofa. She watched him fold his lean and magnificent length into the opposite end. As far away as possible. Which was fine by her!

Despite the defiance that speared from her eyes Sophie paled, her insides churning nauseously. Were her worst fears about to be confirmed? What had he meant when he'd stated that he had no intention of leaving his son with a no-good, sticky-fingered scrubber like her? Or words to that effect!

It was on the tip of her tongue to burst out with accusations of her own. She wasn't a thief. She'd been set up. But accusing his wife—and that sly maid of hers—wouldn't bring any bonus. It would cause mischief—and what was the point of that? Besides, he probably wouldn't believe her in a million years.

Putting him straight on what really mattered, in a voice that aimed for cool determination but merely achieved an anguished croak, she said, 'I suppose I can understand your not wanting to wash your hands of Torry—if I try hard enough,' she amended, to let him know that, knowing what a love-rat he was, she'd expected the complete opposite. 'And I promise you can see him whenever you like—to make sure he's being brought up properly,' she added, with an injection of heavy sarcasm, still stinging from his opinion that she would make a rotten mother. 'Think about it. Publicly acknowledging him would only hurt and humiliate your wife.'

Or wouldn't he care about that either? A prescient shiver juddered its icy way down her spine. And her lush mouth dropped open when he came back smoothly. 'No problem. I don't have a wife.'

Watching the shock register on Sophie's gorgeous features, Ettore wondered how Cinzia would take the news of his newly discovered son. Would she stick with the arrangement he'd coldly and pragmatically agreed to re-enter on the morning after his fantasy woman had shown herself to be a common thief, proving that falling in so-called love was for the birds? Or would she walk away from it? A mental shrug confirmed that as neither of them had emotions invested in their future marriage it didn't matter a damn either way.

The only thing that mattered—would ever matter—was his son. His son. Already showing distinct signs of developing the distinctive Severini features, as he had noted with a fierce stab of pride.

'I won't accept vague visiting rights,' he uttered emphatically. 'Who knows when you might take it into your head to shack up with some other guy, leaving no forwarding address?'

Flaming at that jaundiced view of her lack of morals, Sophie opened her mouth on a vehement protest, but Ettore's hand sliced her to mutinous silence.

'Unfortunately I can't do what I want—what I without doubt could do—and that is gain sole custody of my son. A child needs his mother.'

At that concession Sophie's rock-bottom spirits lifted. Only to plummet down to the sickening depths again as he spelt out with a lethal bite, 'But my son also needs his father. Especially so when his mother appears to have no means of support and, if past records are anything to go on, may be again tempted to resort to theft if her sexual favours don't gather the expected financial rewards.'

Which was what, surely, had happened in

Florence. That was the self-justifying thought that occupied the ensuing stunned silence.

How many times on the island that had become, for him, the earthly embodiment of heaven, had he fantasised over the day when he would be free to lavish on her everything her heart could possibly desire? The mind-deluding plans he'd made—after formally breaking his engagement to Cinzia he would escort his sweet Sophie back to the UK and ask her to be his wife, cover her with kisses and priceless jewels, make his precious darling his for all time.

Some remnant of duty—surviving the enchantment that had turned a tough, analytical business brain to candyfloss—had made him keep his plans to himself until the break with Cinzia had been made. So, with no pay-off in sight that she could see, that witch in an angel's skin had taken the opportunity to lift a valuable piece of jewellery. Her idea of payment due for services rendered!

From being momentarily turned to stone by his hateful low opinion of her Sophie felt anger rage through her with the strength of an out-of-control forest fire. On her lap her small hands clenched into fists and her words hissed through gritted teeth. 'I've never stolen anything in my life! So don't you dare say I have!' Her heart beat heavily against her chestbone in blistering outrage. 'And as you're not married to—to that ghastly woman, I can tell you that she must have planted whatever it was in my case. Or she told that maid of hers to do it!'

Ettore appraised her with unreadable dark-as-night eyes, drawling with cutting sarcasm, 'And why would she do that?'

'Because she's off her rocker!' Sophie, rigid as a broomhandle, shot right back.

Ignoring that off-the-wall scenario, he said smoothly, 'You didn't deny the attempted theft.' He could swear his heart had stopped beating while he'd waited for some believable explanation for the presence of the missing jewel tucked away in her luggage. 'Your final silence was an admission of guilt.'

It would have looked like that, Sophie admitted with weary hindsight, feeling like a pricked balloon. Eyes lowered, she mumbled, 'I was hurting—speechless. It was like a nightmare.' She didn't want to bring it all up, she never wanted to have to think about that traumatic period in her life again, but she had to stand her corner. 'I believed you were the love of my life. And all the time you were lying. All the time you were on the brink of marriage. I only found out that night.' The anguish of that dark memory tightened her voice as she spelled it out. 'I was having trouble trying to come to terms with that. And when you lot barged into my room and accused me of being a thief—well, like I said, my denials might have sounded half-hearted—because I was knocked speechless.'

So put that in your pipe and smoke it, you two-timing, lying rat! was her unspoken bitter thought, smartly switched off as a frustrated bellow from the bedroom invaded her ears.

Torry. A tender smile warmed her features as she rose to go to him on legs that weren't as steady as she would have liked.

Watching her go, his eyes annoyingly fixed on the sway of her jeans-clad nicely rounded behind, Ettore drew his dark brows into a frowning line. So that was how it must have happened. His sister or brother-in-law must have casually mentioned his long-standing engagement. Certainly not Cinzia, because at that time he'd already told her of his change of plan, confessing he'd fallen fathoms deep in love with Sophie.

It hadn't gone as smoothly as he'd expected on the night of Flavia's birthday party. Cinzia had demanded so much of his time to 'talk things through', sounding so reasonable when she'd pointed out that their forthcoming wedding—some time in the future of his choosing—would still be so right, that marrying the hired help would be the biggest mistake of his life. Could he see her entertaining his business associates, arranging glittering functions, holding her own with their set? If he had the hots for her, then by all means he should discreetly get it out of his system, but he mustn't throw away the eminently suitable union of their two great families and all the accruing social and financial benefits.

Cinzia had been right, he'd bitterly acknowledged the next day. Reason went out of the window when a guy was in the throes of a passionate love affair with the wrong woman. So the long-standing engagement had been back on.

Learning of his engagement would have led Sophie to believe that her affair with him had no future. Not bothering to wait and ask him to confirm or deny it, she'd followed her sly, greedy instincts and lifted a piece of valuable jewellery. And now she had the bare-faced cheek to accuse Cinzia of planting it!

He could hear her moving about in the poky kitchen he'd glimpsed off the living area, her voice warm and soothing as she talked to her son.

His son!

On his feet in a nanosecond, Ettore let his long stride carry him through to a kitchen that was the size of a cupboard. She held the wriggling child high on one shoulder while she juggled with a pan and a bottle of baby milk. Ettore's brows crashed down.

Two strong hands fastened around his son's squirming little body as he lifted him into his own arms, ignoring Sophie's disgruntled, 'Hey! What do you think you're doing!' concentrating instead on the way the child's big dark eyes widened as they fixed on his.

Ettore smiled. Torry smiled right back, showing a single white tooth, and reached out chubby hands to grab his father's hair. Ettore grinned unstoppably. He felt almost light-headed with emotion.

'Why didn't you tell me when you knew you were pregnant with my child?' he demanded thickly.

Resisting the possessive instinct to snatch her baby right back again, Sophie got on with what she was doing, her cheeks pink with scorn as she pushed out, 'When I finally realised, as far as I knew you were already married. You wouldn't have wanted to know. That kind of bombshell wouldn't have gone down well with your high-quality new wife! I was perfectly capable of coping alone!'

What she had against Cinzia, Ettore neither knew nor cared. The only time they'd had anything to do with each other had been when Sophie had been shown to be a thief. Resentment at having been found out? Probably. He dismissed the subject, concentrating instead on the outflowing of paternal love for the tiny child he held against his heart.

'But you're not coping, are you?' he pointed out as she assembled the baby bottle. Her hands were unsteady, he noted, without a jot of sympathy.

'I am so.' She kept her voice carefully level, afraid of Torry picking up antagonistic vibes. Sliding the bottle onto what passed for a breakfast bar, she settled herself on the solitary plastic-topped stool and held out her arms for the baby—who, annoyingly, seemed to have taken to the tall dark stranger.

Necessity overcoming his reluctance to hand his child back to such an unfit mother, Ettore obliged, gently placing the firm, warm little body on Sophie's lap. He could have strangled himself for the powerful onslaught of animal lust as the back of one of his hands inadvertently brushed against the underside of one perfectly formed, bountiful breast.

Furious with himself, he paced sharply back until the claustrophobic confines of the space that only an estate agent could have named 'kitchen' brought him in contact with an ancient gas cooker. His hands thrust deep into the pockets of his Savile Row trousers, he enquired with an acid bite, 'So, how do you propose supporting my son? And I warn you, relying on hand-outs from a string of dubious lovers won't cut it.'

Flushed, hot and bothered, Sophie overlooked that highly insulting warning. Someone should have warned her that the brush of his hand against her breast would still be lethal, turning her insides into quivering jelly, shafting wicked sensation directly to the core of her being, making her poor heart pound. He'd been so close as he'd leant over her, the warm tangy male scent of him a powerful aphrodisiac. She gulped thickly, hoping he wasn't noticing the way the almost painfully tight peaks of her breasts were thrusting against her woolly sweater as the last of Torry's milk disappeared into his eager mouth.

What was it about this man? her mind berated. He was, to use a word Nanny Hopkins would have chosen, a cad—and yet just to look at him sent rampant hormones raging all through her stupid body!

In her late teens she'd believed herself in love with Jake. Meeting him at a friend's party, she'd thought he was the cat's whiskers. Disenchantment had only set in when she'd learned that his idea of commitment extended no further than choosing which socks to wear. The only time they'd made love it had had no effect on her, had only made her wonder if this— a painful handful of seconds—was what all the fuss was about.

So what made Ettore Severini so very different? She knew he was a lying creep, yet still—

As Torry made a lunge for the bottle she'd forgotten she was holding she smartly made her mind abandon that line of questioning and got out, as coolly as she could, 'I'm job-hunting, if you must know.'

And into the beat of chilling silence that followed that slice of information her resentment flared and unstoppably spilled out. 'Though, entirely down to you, I'll have to accept something really low paid. But I'll manage—see if I don't!'

'*Basta!*' An impatient hand sliced through the

three feet of space that lay between them. Dark-as-night eyes glittered at her. 'Enough of this pointless waffle. Do you expect me to believe you could earn enough to provide decent accommodation, regular reliable childcare and meet the day-to-day living expenses of you and a child in a city as high cost as this? Get real. If the aim of your spiel about "managing" and "coping" was to disguise your intentions of living off some guy in return for bedroom favours, you've failed abysmally. I will not allow my child to have anything to do with such a sordid situation.'

Sophie's blood turned to ice. Tears of sheer fright spangled in her eyes. He was going to take her baby from her. Everything he'd said pointed that way. She clutched Torry more closely to her. Following Nanny Hopkins's death, and the loss of the little home they'd shared, she had believed that things couldn't get worse.

Wrong.

She was staring at her very worst nightmare. Her eyes flooded.

Ettore smothered a groan. He guessed that turning on the waterworks was a well-honed act, expertly choreographed to make a guy feel a heel. Dismissing the humiliating fact that just for a few moments it had actually worked, that portraying helpless female vulnerability had made him instinctively want to back-pedal, cut the tough male stuff, find a tissue and wipe her eyes, he bit out, 'You have two choices. You and my son return to Italy with me, where you will be provided with a luxurious villa and my son will grow to manhood with every possible advantage—and that includes his father as a permanent fixture. Or you refuse and face a court battle. Which I will win.'

His dark eyes fixed her with arrogant intent. 'Do as I want and you will have a life of luxury and you will keep your son. Go against me and you will lose him. Oh, the court might grant you occasional visiting rights, but with your track record I wouldn't bank on it.' His wide sensual mouth hardened. 'Your choice.'

CHAPTER FIVE

IT HAD been no choice at all.

He had called all the shots. Either option on offer meant that Ettore would have his son. Sophie had no doubt at all that with his financial clout and high-status family background, not to mention his own forceful personality and the list of the sins she'd been landed with, which he could produce at will, he would win the most fiercely fought custody battle.

The third option that had wildly occurred to her, to tell him to go right ahead and take her to court, and then take Torry and do a runner, had been reluctantly dismissed as being plain selfish, not to mention downright stupid. He would have tracked her down. And in the meantime what sort of life would Torry have had on the run? And when he found them—as, given his limitless resources, he surely would—he'd have another big black mark to hold against her.

So she had given in for the sake of her son. Had meekly allowed them to be torn away from London and transported—in the sort of style and luxury that made her eyes goggle—around the major capitals of Europe for a full month, conscious that Ettore was dead set on keeping them—Torry especially—where he could see them for all but the few hours it took him to conduct his no-doubt extremely important business.

He had an ego the size of a barrage balloon, she had decided, not for the first time, and it suited him to have the cowed little woman trudging along in his kingly wake. Her sense of self-worth had gone underground, and the only murmur of dissent coming from her mostly held tongue had issued when on their first stopover—Paris for five days—she'd been presented with the nanny he'd hired for Torry.

'Torry doesn't need a nanny! I can look after him myself,' she'd muttered on a fierce undertone, as Nanny had taken herself off to the adjacent hotel suite to unpack and settle in. She'd had nothing against the highly referenced, plain, obviously competent and kindly Minette personally, but she refused to be sidelined.

But he'd come back at her in the smoothly detached tone he'd used to her ever since she'd agreed to return to Italy with him. 'It is expected. For a son of mine not to have the best, highly trained professional care available would raise eyebrows. That aside, I personally demand the best for him.'

So what did that make her? Fourth rate? The bottom of the heap? Incensed, and still in that furious undertone, she'd ripped back at him, 'Not only am I his mother, I'm a highly trained nanny, too! Or I was until you made it impossible for me to work in that field again! Or had you forgotten?'

His insulting response had been to look through her, turn on the heels of his hand-made shoes and walk out of her suite and back to his.

So here they were at last, at his luxuriously spacious villa deep in the unspoiled Tuscan countryside, having collected enough baggage to break several dozen camels' backs.

Clothing and toys for Torry, which his father had picked out with loving enthusiasm, and enough designer gear to clothe a dozen catwalk models for a year for her. Plus newly shaped hair, wildly expensive make-up and perfumes. Not that he'd had much of a hand in that, apart from paying the horrendous bills. He'd hired personal shoppers—definitely hands-off where she was concerned. The desire to please, pamper and spoil her wasn't taking up a millimetre of space in his mind; the need to ensure that the mother of his son didn't disgrace the family name by any hint of second-hand shabbiness was to the forefront.

A sigh dredging through her, Sophie turned from her contemplation of the Tuscan night sky, spangled with stars, slowly letting the drapes fall back to close out the cool March night.

The long evening yawned ahead. What to do? Silly question. The same as on each of the other week's worth of evenings since they'd arrived at the luxurious hill villa and Ettore had taken off somewhere unspecified. Sit in this elegant drawing room trying to read until it was time to take herself off to bed.

She felt like a spare part. Useless.

There was a housekeeper, a cook, a daily maid of all work, and a brace of gardeners to tend the beautiful grounds. She didn't have to lift a finger. The only real stand she'd made was to insist that she and she alone cared for her baby while he was awake, and took him in his brand-new buggy for his twice-daily airings.

If this was to be the norm there would have to be changes, she vowed, her small chin at a defiant angle. So much for Ettore's pious spoutings on the subject of his son needing both his parents—he'd taken off at speed as soon as he'd ushered them over the threshold!

Possessive, or what? Torry was his son, and unfortunately she came with the package. So he'd shut them away out of sight where no one who hadn't been thoroughly vetted could have anything to do with his child—especially not all those imaginary lovers he'd lined up for her in his warped, highly inventive imagination!

Close to spitting bricks, Sophie felt her mood suddenly change. Did she really want Ettore as a close part of her son's life? Around most of the time? It would be unbearable. Around him she felt... Felt what?

But that didn't bear thinking about either, because she'd be lying to herself if she pretended she didn't know exactly what she felt around him. Sheer animal lust. Crazy. She was disgusted with herself. She no longer loved him—of course she didn't—and she didn't trust him an inch! So why did her wretched body come alive so vibrantly when he was around?

Resolutely she pushed him out of her mind, picked up the thriller she'd been trying to read for the last few evenings and opened it. From the position of the bookmark it seemed she'd got to page thirty, but she couldn't remember a single word.

Ettore drove between the tall cypresses that bordered the drive up to the villa feeling all wired up, as if a high-voltage electric current was fizzing through his bloodstream. He couldn't understand it. He should be feeling relaxed. The tough part was over.

Winning Mama over when it came to a surprise grandson had been a doddle. She couldn't wait to see him, hold him—and what sort of name was Torry? A contraction of Ettore, obviously!

The darling newest addition to the Severini family must be brought to Venice at once, for a proper christening. The Barsini family would politely turn a blind eye to his lapse, and Cinzia would accept the child, she was sure. The advantages of the forthcoming union were too great to be jeopardised over one little slip.

As for the baby's mother—she didn't want details of his affair, too tiresome—she couldn't stay indefinitely at his country villa, of course. A small apartment in Florence, perhaps? An allowance? Wasn't that how men conducted these things? And had he heard the gossip? Signor di Barsini had been involved in some catastrophic investments. Though she didn't believe a word of it...

As always, Ettore had allowed his adored mother's prattle to wash over him. He had heard no such rumour. He'd check it out. Marriage to Cinzia was now out of the question, but he'd help if he could, if it was needed.

He would do what he had to do and, as always, Mama would eventually accept it and claim it had been her idea in the first place. Dropping a kiss on her powdery cheek, he had presented her with his gift of her favourite perfume and taken her to lunch.

His sister had been a different matter. The newest

member of the family presented no problem, but the child's mother *was* a problem.

'I really took to her,' Flavia had said. 'Wonderful with the children, such fun—they both adored her. But she knew when to be firm. We all respected her, and I got really fond of her in the few months she was with us. I felt physically sick when she turned out to be a thief—it showed what a poor judge of character I was. You too, if you went far enough to get her pregnant. Do you really think you can handle that?'

He could handle anything. Ettore mentally reinforced that statement of fact as he garaged his car. Even the knowledge that in order to make his son legitimate he would have to marry a common little thief who would give her body to any man she thought she could get something out of.

His stomach twisted in an angry knot. If she'd had a little more patience on that fateful night she would have learned that, his formal breaking with Cinzia over, he would walk barefoot to the ends of the world for her, that he adored her, was begging her to be his wife. He would have married her without knowing what she really was and suffered a devastating blow when he'd found out that she viewed him as nothing more than a meal ticket.

His jaw tightened. He'd got over it, hadn't he?

This way would be better, he assured himself as he let himself in by the main door and made his presence known to his housekeeper. Sophie Lang had already fallen from the pedestal he'd put her on with a resounding crash.

Knowing what she was, he wouldn't be in any

position to suffer a future knock-out blow, and he would keep a strict eye on her to make sure she didn't stray, was never even tempted to. They'd be good in bed. He'd make it so good she'd never think of looking at another man. And this time his emotions wouldn't be involved. Been there, done that, learned the lesson.

Loyal to her fingertips, his housekeeper hadn't raised an eyebrow when he'd arrived with his surprise entourage a week ago. His son, his son's English mother and a French nanny. And now she blandly informed him, when asked, that Miss Lang was in the first-floor salon with the tray of tea she'd just had delivered.

Cinzia had taken his news just as expected, given the cold pride that was the dominant part of her character. And he congratulated himself as he took the stairs up to the nursery suite, complacently putting his wired-up feeling down to the prospect of seeing his son again after a whole week away.

He'd been feeling bad about letting Cinzia down after such a long engagement. Especially when the last time they'd dined together, prior to his departure for his London branch, she'd remarked idly, 'I suppose we should think about naming the day. Not that I'm pushing you, of course. No rush as far as I'm concerned. We both accept that our marriage will be a financial and highly successful social arrangement—it's not as though we can't wait to get our hands on each other, or anything so crass.' She'd given the tinkling laugh that was beginning to irritate him more each time he heard it. 'But Papa's getting a touch impatient. So give it some thought while you're away.'

Anxious to formally tie the Barsini and Severini fortunes together. Ettore could easily understand that. Cinzia's father wasn't getting any younger. Naturally he would be pushing for their union.

Remembering his mother's mention of gossip about the di Barsini financial difficulties, when he'd seen Cinzia he'd probed gently, 'Mama says there are rumours that your father is in financial difficulties. Tell me, is there any truth in them?'

Her denial had been immediate and emphatic, but his conscience had been pricking him when he'd then broken the news of his son's existence to his about-to-be-dumped fiancée.

He'd been immediately salved by her, 'If you think I'd marry you and share my home with your bastard, you must be mad! I'd be a laughing stock!'

That that scenario had never been on his agenda was something he hadn't bothered to mention. He had just endured her ongoing shrill outrage because it was the least he could do in the circumstances.

'And even if you keep your bastard hidden away somewhere in Italy the secret's bound to get out. People will snigger behind my back. I refuse to be put in that position! You should have washed your hands of it. Got it adopted or something. Or left the mother to get on with it. Discretion—we agreed, remember? Not siring bastards all over the place and flaunting them! So until you get it out of our lives, consider the engagement off! I'll reconsider when you've sent them both packing to the other side of the earth!'

'My son stays with me,' he'd imparted formally, appalled by this shrewish side of her he'd never seen before. He'd put it down to shock, gently pointing out that the cold-blooded arrangement they'd entered into had been a monumental mistake, that brainwashing offspring into following outdated ideas of family duty should be classified as a mortal sin. 'You are a beautiful woman, Cinzia. One day you will find someone you can love. I wasn't that man, but one day you will find him, and he will truly love you. You deserve more than a union of financial and social convenience.'

Putting aside the memory of that final interview, he lost track of the time he spent gazing down at his sleeping son, the self-admittedly fatuous grin on his face to be replaced by a slashing frown when, on calling in on Nanny in the adjacent room, he learned that *bébé* Torry now had another tooth and had begun to crawl.

Milestones in his son's life—and missed. A short week ago he'd got around—admittedly at speed—by shuffling on his bottom and chortling. Now he could crawl!

Madonna diavola, he would not miss any more!

Getting to the first-floor salon took him only a matter of rigid-shouldered seconds, with the tension inside him building to massive proportions.

If his son's mother had truly been the angel she'd so cleverly hoodwinked him into believing she was then there would have been no problem. She would have been everything he'd wanted and more—much more.

Hot hatred for the fact that she was the opposite

of the angel he had so besottedly once believed her to be made his brain hurt and his heart clench. Cool it, he commanded the unwanted physical reaction to an emotion he'd confidently believed over and long forgotten.

The course he had set himself to follow was the right one. For his son. He'd accepted the idea of a loveless marriage with Cinzia—with a few mental kicks—for outmoded dynastic reasons. He could take a loveless marriage to his son's mother in his stride, and make sure the flaws in her character, which were huge, didn't get to gape any wider.

Marginally calmed by that slice of common sense, he pushed the door open and walked in.

And his heart stopped beating. Then raced on. A rosy flush had stolen over her entrancing features at his entry, the huge grey eyes widening, her long throat convulsing as she swallowed back what he took to be a gasp of surprise. Such a delicate throat…the purity of its lines revealed by the deep V neckline of the dress she was wearing. Something soft and silky of a deep misty blue that made all that long blonde hair look like spun platinum.

A surge of lust as powerful as the one that had so comprehensively shattered him on that distant beach on that distant night had him fighting for control over the tempestuous, treacherous torrent. So his voice, when he finally got the words out, didn't emerge as he'd intended—smooth and cool as polished ebony—but on a harsh rasp that made his statement, even to his own ears, seem almost obscene.

'I've decided to marry you. It's the only way you

get a life of luxury and I get my son. Fall in line and we both get what we want.'

The moment the insensitively put statement of intent was out Ettore suffered an acutely sharp attack of conscience and self-loathing—a condition so new to him it took his breath away.

Her face turned the colour of skimmed milk and the book she'd been holding dropped to her lap as her fingertips flew up to cover her mouth, and he wished the unfeeling words unsaid.

She was the mother of his child, and despite past sins she deserved better than a proposal that had come out like a threat. A good, loving mother, as he'd been at pains to note. It now hit him that she was vulnerable too, transported against her will away from everything and everyone she knew. She would be on the defensive, and persuading her to do the right and sensible thing for their son's sake would take gentle coaxing.

Sophie gulped around the painful constriction in her throat and shoved out a rather wobbly 'no', sickeningly aware that there had been a time when she would have crawled over hot coals to accept his proposal of marriage, no matter how coldly put.

But not like this. She didn't want an empty life of pampered, idle luxury. She wanted love. And trust. And that was not on offer—never had been as far as he was concerned, she acknowledged wearily, wrapping her arms around her slender body to hold herself together.

'I could have put that better,' he acknowledged gently, taking the paces necessary to bring him to where she sat, as if turned to stone.

He took both her hands within his and pulled her unresisting body to her feet. The warmth of her, the perfume she was wearing, filled him with sudden raw need. He had been without a woman for far too long. In fact he'd lost interest in the opposite sex since this amoral little temptress had revealed her true colours, he calculated with unpleasant surprise.

Ettore clamped his jaw, denying the insistent throb of desire that bade him take those lush soft lips and kiss her senseless, and managed, with a smoothness that belied his ragged thoughts, 'I'm not asking for a knee-jerk response. If we marry, our son will have a stable family life. He will be legitimate—not my mistress's bastard.'

Sophie dragged her hands from his. This close to his magnificent body she was horribly tempted to agree to anything he said. But... 'Who said anything about my being your mistress?' she shot at him, delicate colour flooding her cheeks, making her huge eyes sparkle.

Two unthinking steps away from him had her sprawling back in the chair so recently vacated. The breath escaped her lungs on a shaky gust. If he thought that housing her beneath his roof, doling out the food she ate and the clothes on her back, gave him any rights at all over her body then he'd have to think again. Her weak body might crave him but self-preservation firmly reminded her that she could easily fall in love with him all over again. And that would lead to even more heartbreak and misery.

A beat of silence as he stuffed his hands into the pockets of the superbly cut trousers of his immaculate dark business suit. His wilfully passionate mouth had a wryly sardonic twist as he rocked slightly back on his heels and pointed out in a tone of unarguable reason, 'Between us we have made a beautiful child. You and he are under my protection. We will be living together, in my home. Whether we avoid each other like the plague or spend every opportunity writhing between the sheets is of no consequence. People will draw their own conclusions—that you are my kept woman, my mistress. And they will brand our son a bastard. Is that what you want for him?'

Hating the stark truth of that, Sophie squirmed. 'Then let me take Torry back to England,' she shot at him. 'Avoid unpleasant gossip. No one I know would be so outdated and downright hypocritical as to hold the fact that my baby was born out of wedlock against him! You can visit him whenever you like, and there won't be a snob in sight to turn a hair!'

'Not an option,' he uttered brutally, his patience fast dwindling—because he wanted to kiss her into compliance. His whole body burned and tautened with the need to stamp her with his ownership, to know again the shattering ecstasy of having her soft, all-woman, wildly responsive body beneath his.

She was the mother of his child; ergo she was his woman, warts and all! Quelling the unworthy desire, he forced himself to find and hold onto a reasonable tone. 'Put the welfare of our son first and think about my proposal. No immediate hurry. Just weigh up the advantages. And in the meantime—' the sudden grin that lit up his unforgettably handsome features made her shudder with the usual devastating reaction '—I suggest we start getting to know each other. Very thoroughly.'

CHAPTER SIX

'STARTING now?'

One winged ebony brow was urbanely elevated, and a slow smile curved his sinfully beautiful male mouth as long fingers unknotted the pale grey silk tie from the collar of his pristine white shirt with deft deliberation.

A heart that had picked up the wild speed of sheer panic rendered Sophie speechless. So she couldn't coolly announce, *Forget it. I'm tired and going to bed*, as she would have liked. She would have got up and walked from the room if she'd thought her legs had a snowflake's chance in hell of holding her upright—but she knew they hadn't.

His stunning eyes, sliding languorously from the crown of her smooth blonde head to the toes of her extravagantly expensive shoes, mesmerised her. Told her he'd meant 'getting to know each other' in the carnal sense.

Gulping shakily, Sophie felt her breasts peak with almost painful anticipation and surge against the fine silk of her dress. The way he was undoing the top buttons of his shirt was nothing short of downright erotic. Any moment now he would casually dispose of the suit jacket that clothed his honed, blow-your-mind-sexy physique with such fluid elegance.

She squirmed. Her breath shortened. Her tummy tightened on a spiral of renewed panic—and some-

90

thing else she was too ashamed to identify. If he moved towards her and—heaven forbid—touched her, she'd be utterly lost. His to take his pleasure on. And she would give it back with interest, just as she'd mindlessly done before. She was too honest to kid herself otherwise. Where he was concerned she had as much self-discipline as a lump of putty.

But having sex without deep emotional commitment would make her hate herself. Having sex without the cement of love would never be for her.

That the sex with him had been truly almost unbelievably wonderful once was undeniable. When she'd loved him so. She had no argument with that. But then she'd believed him to be the most fabulous creature ever created. Endlessly considerate, utterly charming, warm and passionate. Loving. Addictively sexy. All an act, a perfectly honed exercise in effortless seduction.

Now she knew him for what he really was: coldly autocratic, unfeeling, distrustful, all held together with a thread of cruelty. She loathed him. She absolutely did!

Yet, perversely, she still wanted him like crazy!

The jacket removed, he smiled that very male smile. Sophie pulled a ragged breath into her already hopelessly shaky lungs. The wide shoulders beneath the fine cotton white shirt owed not a thing to any top-of-the-range tailor's discreet padding.

As she already knew. Because she knew every inch of that lithe, sexy body. As he knew every inch of hers. Inches he was now reappraising with avid intensity.

Dazed grey eyes followed the slow sweep of his

much darker gaze, and her throat went dry as fiery heat pooled between her thighs. She knew he was reading all the signs she was incapable of hiding.

Cursing the unwanted rush of hormones that invaded her helpless body whenever he was around, she had to force herself to stay sane, hovering between savage disappointment and a bone-weakening rush of relief when he hooked the discarded suit jacket over one shoulder and drawled, 'On consideration, it's late. We'll leave it until the morning.' And sauntered out.

Another glorious Tuscan spring morning. Sophie crawled out of bed, her limbs feeling as if they belonged to someone else, her head throbbing, eyelids gritty.

A largely sleepless night. Tossing. Turning. His harshly delivered, unbelievably awful proposal of marriage running rings in her weary brain.

Marry him? As if she would!

She could see where he was coming from. Of course she could. She wasn't completely stupid. If he was married to her, the new found son he was so unexpectedly possessive of would bear his name. Every facet of her child's upbringing would be his to direct exactly as he felt fit, with her own wishes deemed of no account whatsoever—as witness the hiring of Nanny. And that little cruel charade he'd staged last night had been to make sure he could still turn her on if he wanted to. He wouldn't want a wife who gave him a slap in the eye whenever he could be bothered to go to her bed!

So—bingo! Got her! Got a willing body to use

whenever he felt like it, an addict of what he could do to her. Keep her compliant and clingy, all the time cynically despising her for her weakness, for her supposed many faults—while he got exactly what he wanted.

Her stomach rolled as she wondered wildly how she could handle the coming day, then guilty conscience dealt a hammer blow. Grabbing her aqua satin robe, she cursed herself for letting him monopolise her thoughts. This was the first time ever she hadn't leapt from bed at Torry's first wakening holler.

Bare feet cringing on the cold marble floor tiles, she flew to the nursery, one door down the corridor from her suite, to find she was redundant. She could have stayed in bed all day and everything would have proceeded like clockwork.

Ettore was sprawled out in the nursing chair, the sunlight streaming in through the partly opened window making his tousled hair gleam like a raven's wing. Tousled because Torry, bouncing on his knee, was grabbing handfuls and squealing, happy as a sandboy, and the unwanted, resented French nanny was tidying up his discarded night things and breakfast pots in the background, radiating an aura of kindly, comfortable, quiet efficiency.

Surplus to requirements. A spare part. Not needed.

The energy that had brought her sprinting into the room drained from Sophie's body in a sickening flood. Would she ever be able to assert herself in the face of this totally dominant male who always got exactly what he wanted?

The answer was given when he finally noticed her

presence and remarked blandly, 'Get dressed. We'll take Torry for an airing. We'll take a picnic breakfast with us. Main door in twenty minutes.' Dismissing her entirely, he gave his undivided, doting attention back to the bouncing baby, who seemed as besotted with the father as the father was with the son.

On automatic pilot, and utterly miserable, Sophie returned to her room and showered and dressed, in classy cream-coloured linen pants and a tawny silk knit short-sleeved top which clung like a lover's touch to every curve of her bountiful breasts.

Awful! Her cheeks flamed with disgust—not with the classy top but with her body. She dragged it off and stuffed it back in a drawer. After her undisguised physical response the night before he would be bound to think she was flaunting herself, begging for his attention! She couldn't help the shape of her body, could she? But at least she could disguise it.

The puppy fat that had brought forth uncomplimentary, cringe-making remarks and unkind jokes from her stepmother and stepsister during her unenviable teenage years had mostly melted away, but it had left her with still too much bounty both north and south of her gratifyingly tiny waist.

Fingers flying through the contents of the spacious hanging cupboard, she found what she was looking for. A slate-grey silk shirt. Meant to be worn, so the personal shopper had informed her in Paris—or had it been Milan?—with the sleeves rolled up, casually unbuttoned to cleavage level, tucked into the white silk harem pants that languished amongst all the other stuff in the crammed cupboard, and with a scarlet silk scarf knotted round her waist.

She left the shirt hanging loose, hopefully disguising the difference between north, south and middle, buttoned the cuffs at the wrist, buttoned the front firmly up to her throat. Worn thus, it did nothing for her. Good!

A smear of moisturiser was her only make-up; her hair she scooped back and scalp-tinglingly tied with a length of ribbon. The pressing need for self-assertion firmly lodged in her brain now, Sophie strode purposefully down the broad sweeping staircase into the huge, airy entrance hall.

There was no point in simply feeling miserable at the situation she found herself in, or giving up. She had to be firm, fight her own corner, let Ettore Severini know he couldn't call all the shots.

Only to find herself going weak at the knees and definitely breathless when she saw him on the sunlit sweep of gravel in front of the beautiful house. Designer casuals clothed his powerful frame with smooth sophistication, and the warm spring sunlight threw those hard cheekbones, the aristocratic blade of his nose and the beautiful mouth that was now set in a slightly mocking line, into heartstopping prominence. He had never looked more handsome.

One brown hand held the bar of Torry's pushchair; the other, extended in her direction, offered a compact wicker picnic hamper.

Hauling herself together, doing her utmost to avoid those compelling dark eyes, Sophie ignored the hamper and fastened both slender hands on the pushchair. Bag-carrier she would not be—not while he took charge of her precious baby!

Setting off at a breathless pace down the long cypress-shaded drive, the tot-sized filmy parasol fluttering, shading Torry from the beat of the sun, Sophie headed off across a sweeping expanse of emerald-green grass.

'This is the way we normally come.' She tossed a belated explanation for her manic behaviour over her shoulder. Ettore was following, doubtless frowning his displeasure over the graceless way she was wearing the designer clothes that must have cost him a bomb.

Let him! She didn't care what he thought—just as long as he didn't get it into his too-handsome head that she was making an effort with her appearance for him! She couldn't afford to give him any encouragement in the seduction department—not when he was too darn difficult to resist!

And she had taken charge, hadn't she? It should have made her feel good. But it didn't. A huge lump of heavy hopelessness was lodged in her chest. Only she wasn't going to think of why that should be.

Her apparently rock-solid antagonism crumbled away as they reached the spot that was her all-time favourite, discovered on Torry's daily airings.

A flight of shallow stone steps led down to idyllic perfumed seclusion, an intimate circle of grass bordered by the flowers of quince, pink and white, and smoky lavender-tinted lilac bushes, all underplanted with dusky, sweet-scented violets. Tuscan spring in all its jewelled glory, working its insidious magic.

Gently negotiating the buggy down the steps, pointedly ignoring Ettore's immediate offer of assistance, she headed for the comfy wooden bench seat beneath an arbour of white jasmine.

Parking the buggy, she bent to lift Torry high into her arms, drinking in the sweetly soft baby scent of him, the touch of his velvety skin against her face. He began to wriggle. She knew he recognised where they were and, obliging, she put him down on the short smooth grass and watched him excitedly crawl away in ever-increasing circles. She savoured the brief moment as peaceful contentment filled her, honestly admitting that her baby would never have known this kind of freedom, the benison of clean country air, back in Tim's London flat. At least as far as Torry's wellbeing was concerned she'd done the right thing, and as for herself—well, she'd have to cope somehow.

But there was a very unsettling sensation deep in her stomach as Ettore's long tanned fingers fastened around her arm and he drew her down beside him on the wooden bench. Her pulses jumped at his nearness. Even seated a few inches away, as he fondly watched his son's blue romper-clad rump bobbing about in the dappled sunlight, she could feel his body heat. It was decidedly unnerving.

If he was going to broach the subject of marriage again she would gather Torry and walk away, leaving him in no doubt that she would never agree in a month of Sundays. But he didn't. A soft smile curving that mouth to die for, he asked gently, 'Why Torry? It's not a name I've come across before.'

From the flash of bright colour that flooded her cheeks at his lazily couched question Ettore knew he had hit a raw spot. Good. His aim was to get to know what made her the woman she was. If she was to be his wife—and she was; for his son's sake he would entertain no doubt on that score—then he had to delve deep into her psyche. He knew very little about her background except that she'd lost her mother at a very young age. He'd been too besotted, too involved with the immediacy of earth-shattering physical attraction on the island, to have any spare time for sharing personal confidences.

He slid his arm across the back of the seat behind her and saw her tense. He wasn't going to touch her, but wryly admitted that he wanted to. His fingers were itching to remove the scrap of ribbon that held her glorious hair starkly back from her face, to drift through the luxurious silkiness. Whatever her failings, criminal activities amongst them, he couldn't deny their sexual chemistry.

Once it had made a besotted fool of him, but this time round he had his brain in gear. He would call all the shots. He simply needed to know what had made her into the kind of woman she was. Having the salient facts—maybe even rooting out mitigating circumstances—would make having her in his life easier. Getting rid of her completely wasn't an option. Not while Torry needed both parents.

Firmly resisting the impulse to touch her—he could control animal lust when he wanted to, couldn't he?—he reminded himself that last night he'd decided to take his time over prising information out of her. Go at it like a bull at a gate and she'd clam up, and he would never learn her secrets. Finding out what made her what she was more important than assuaging a sexual itch.

Besides, from the signals she'd displayed last night—the flush of colour across her delicate cheekbones, the shortening of her breath, the give-away peaking of those luscious breasts—he was confident that he could take her any time he wanted, persuade her that great sex, unlimited luxury, was a fair exchange for giving him what he really wanted. Parental rights over his son.

Pushing away the uncomfortable feeling that care for his son, flesh of his flesh, was a laudable emotion but his means of making it happen were undoubtedly questionable, he reminded her softly of his question. 'Well?'

Sophie gulped, her throat convulsing. Impossible not to tell the truth—it took a very nimble mind to come up with a really convincing lie just like that—so she got out woodenly, 'I named him for his father. Shortened to Torry. Okay?'

Very okay—despite that final note of embarrassed defiance. He'd known it already. He'd have been totally stupid not to make the connection. At least she'd answered him honestly. Something warm curled around his heart, much to his surprise. Probably down to the fact that despite erroneously writing him off as a bottomless source of goodies all that time ago, and helping herself to Cinzia's property, she hadn't forgotten him completely—not if she'd named their baby for him, he supposed.

There were more questions—one in particular was puzzling him—but they could wait. Withdrawing his arm, determined to get her to relax, he opened the hamper, withdrew a silver-plated Thermos, poured hot coffee into a bone china mug and handed it to her.

'Help yourself to what you want.' Ettore shifted

along the bench and placed the open hamper between them. 'While I prevent our son from eating the violets. He has a very inquisitive nature, yes?'

The warmth of his smile solidified the breath in her lungs. Her throat convulsed. When he turned on the charm she had about as much backbone as a jellyfish! Acidly wondering what he was up to, she watched him lope across the lawn towards Torry, who was now trying to eat his sunhat. Guessing that bully-boy tactics weren't going to work had he decided to turn on the charm? Charm her into agreeing to be his wife and then, that accomplished, reveal his true nature by showing how much he despised her— or what he trenchantly believed she was—ignoring her until he felt the urge for a female to share his bed?

Well, it wouldn't work! Once a cheat, always a cheat. Had Cinzia, the woman he'd been engaged to, had supposedly loved, found out somehow that he'd been unfaithful and called the wedding off? She didn't suppose she would ever know. But there was no way she would tie herself into such a demeaning union, with a serial womaniser to boot, she vowed, her eyes fixed on him. He'd scooped Torry up into his arms and was now tickling his fat little tummy to chortles of baby laughter.

Drat him for all that wretched charisma! Torry obviously adored him—Torry, who hadn't come into contact with adult males in his short life, had viewed Tim with wide-eyed wariness, clinging to her like a limpet when he, their temporary rescuer, had offered to hold him while she had attempted, one-handed, to fill his plastic baby bath with warm water.

Unlike before, at the start of their passionate affair, she now knew that Ettore's effortless charm, the warm smiles and gentle words, delivered in that spine-tingling, lightly accented voice, were just a well-polished technique to be turned on at will to get what he wanted. So she was immune. Wasn't she?

Of course she was. Ignoring the sigh that seemed to swell up from the soles of her feet, Sophie gave her belated attention to the contents of the hamper. Her stomach growled as she selected a slice of focaccia filled with creamy soft cheese and salami wrapped in a linen napkin and bit into it hungrily. No point in behaving like a Victorian maiden who had lost the love of her life and was going gracefully into a decline! She had his number, and she wouldn't let herself be seduced, cajoled or charmed into again believing that they could have a worthwhile relationship.

No way!

She had absentmindedly started on the luscious purple grapes when Ettore fastened his sleepy son into his buggy, adjusted the parasol and gently wheeled him into the shade cast by a blowsily blossoming white lilac. Sophie was sure the heady perfume must have narcotic qualities, she felt so relaxed and at ease, even able to give a soft, contented smile when Ettore sat beside her.

His mesmeric dark eyes were teasing as he noted the greatly depleted contents of the hamper and commented, 'I hate skinny women who pick at two lettuce leaves and half a radish. I'm glad to see you're not a member of the great dieting army!'

'Even if I get really fat?' Sophie handed him a

linen-wrapped portion of focaccia, not minding the banter. Not now she'd worked out where he was coming from. Besides, always being on the defensive got to be exhausting.

'Not fat. I can think of a better description.' His eyes gleamed wickedly beneath dense dark lashes. 'Delectable, delicious, desirable.'

Sophie closed her eyes and leant back. She wasn't impressed by that old flannel! Desirable? More like a useful commodity to be used if he was in the mood and more sophisticated social equals weren't immediately available! She was getting the hang of being cynical, she decided, amused, at least where Ettore Severini was concerned.

He had once desired her—stuck on that island with no other prey in sight—and look where that had got her! But she'd do it all again, suffer the excruciating pain and humiliation he'd dealt her, because the end result had been her beautiful baby son, whom she loved more than life itself.

A sudden chilly breeze gusted, moulding her shirt to her breasts, and the intimate touch of his lips on her softly parted mouth was like a bolt of lightning, sending electric currents through her bloodstream, making her feel giddy and disorientated.

Hands raised to push him away even while her treacherous mouth clung greedily to his, and she was only brought back to her addled senses by a grumbly whimper from the buggy.

'What was that for?' she demanded crossly, deeply annoyed by the feverish hunger she couldn't in all honesty hide from herself.

Jumping to her feet, she found her legs disgracefully unsteady. She knew her face was scarlet, and wanted to hit him for immediately standing up with her, too close, making her far too aware of the hard, muscular strength of his lean body, and for saying, with a curl of seduction, 'You had cream cheese on your top lip. I couldn't resist. I'm still hungry.' The sinful gleam in his dark eyes told her exactly what he was hungry for, torturing her.

'Then finish the fruit!' she snapped, forgetting to be cool and laid back in the turmoil he'd just created. 'I'm taking Torry inside.'

'Of course.' He fell in step beside her, thrust the hamper at her and lifted the buggy up the steps, striding up them as if his burden weighed no more than a feather, leaving her scurrying to catch up. 'The Tramontano blows straight from the frigid alps. A Tuscan early spring is like a beautiful woman. She blows hot; she blows cold.' A dark brow quirked. 'Just as you do, *cara mia*. You show bad temper because you don't like yourself for enjoying my kiss. I wonder why that is?'

About to offer a vehement denial, Sophie bit the words back. He'd know she was lying, so why bother? He couldn't have failed to notice how her whole body had leapt to life as he'd deepened that tasting of her lips to full-blooded plunder.

'It is a puzzle. Once you panted for my kisses—in the most flattering and delightful way—and very much more, if my memory serves. Now you like to pretend your panting-for-me days are over and throw—what is the current phrase?—a hissy fit if I come near you. It is a riddle I mean to solve.'

Given her dubious track record, he'd imagined that

she'd leap with unseemly haste at his offer of marriage and the pampered lifestyle that went with it.
He'd spoken lightly, teasingly, about solving that
particular riddle, but he'd never been more serious.
The enigma was actually bugging him.

As the villa came into sight Sophie breathed a sigh
of relief. Escape! Surely he could find something to
do other than follow her and Torry around all day.
She was far too susceptible where his all-too-male
animal magnetism was concerned.

Her distinctly perturbed mind was further soothed
when, reaching the main hall, he took the hamper
from her and imparted, 'Paperwork and phone calls
will occupy me for the rest of the day.' But her mental processes were sent haywire again when he tacked
on smoothly, 'We will eat out this evening—the local
trattoria—so wear something casual. It is time you
got to know something of the area. It is not good for
you to be confined to the grounds.'

To hide her dismay Sophie busied herself extract-
ing the sleepy infant from the buggy. An intimate
dinner was a definite no-no. It would remind her too
forcibly of those late suppers they'd eaten beneath
the stars on the island—and, more to the point, of
what had followed.

Coming up with the only get-out she could think
of, she veiled her eyes. 'I couldn't possibly. I have
a baby, remember?' And, if he still didn't get it, she
raised her head and looked him straight in the eye,
pushing home the duties of parenthood. 'I have a
baby alarm in my room should he wake and need
changing—or want a drink.'

'So does Nanny. Have a baby alarm.'

Those fascinating eyes were lit with gentle amusement and his voice softened as he—unforgivably, in Sophie's tremulous opinion—drifted the backs of his lean fingers across her pinkened cheeks.

'That is why she was hired, *cara*. Not to take all care of your child from you, but to allow you to spend the quality time with him, which you both need, while she looks after the more boring side of things—laundry duties, clearing up, babysitting and so on. So that as his mother you are content and not deprived of any outside interests or freedoms.'

His hand dropped back to his side, leaving Sophie feeling weirdly bereft, and open-mouthed at the worrying thought that he actually meant what he said, that he hadn't—as she had initially believed—installed Nanny Minette to distance her from her baby.

Don't be nice to me! she shouted inside her head. Please don't!

And she lacked the spare thought capacity to object when he told her, 'Be ready at eight-thirty,' turned on his heels and strolled away, the angle of his dark head and the set of his wide shoulders displaying the supreme confidence of the alpha male.

CHAPTER SEVEN

SURPRISING herself, Sophie found her mood was quite definitely upbeat, despite the uncomfortable situation she found herself in. Changed and ready, she headed for the nursery and looked in on her sleeping son. Tucked up in the fancy cot Ettore had provided he looked adorable, one tiny hand curved around the fluffy blue teddy that went everywhere with him. Her heart blossomed with love.

Her voice low, she stated, 'He should sleep right through, and we shouldn't be away for long, Minette.'

It was the first time she'd addressed the Nanny by her forename, not being sure whether it was the done thing in a household belonging to a member of the boot-lickable Severini family, and not caring either, because it sounded more friendly. Now that Ettore had actually promised that the Frenchwoman hadn't been expressly hired to form a solid wall between her baby and herself, she found herself relieved to be able to like her.

Minette turned from the blue and cream painted hanging cupboard, folding the minuscule garments destined for the fitted shelves, her homely face beaming. 'All will be well, *madame*. Just relax and enjoy your evening. And may I say how nice you look? I can recognise a Paris designer label when I see one!'

Actually, the soft suede honey-coloured skirt suit

carried a top-flight Italian label, but Sophie wouldn't have hurt the older woman's feelings by disabusing her for the world. So she simply smiled her wide, infectious smile, said thank you, and drifted out of the nursery on kitten heels, trailing subtle fragrance.

Getting ready for an evening that promised the torment of being with a man she loathed and lusted after in equal measure, a man who could turn her on and swipe through her defences with one flicker of a disgracefully long eyelash, a man she also had the inclination to hit with a brick, she'd had a monumental and enlightening change of direction.

Her personal situation needn't be all bad, not if she really worked on it. Ettore might have shown himself to be the sort of man she despised—the sort of man who would seduce his social inferior, speaking of eternal love and all that stuff while being on the brink of marriage to a blue-blooded, filthy rich and beautiful snob—but he hadn't actually married the vile Cinzia di Barsini. He was a free man now. Not engaged to anyone else, as far as she knew, and for some reason that seemed to make things easier.

Besides, a man who could take the tiny son he hadn't known he had straight to his heart, treat him like a little prince, take his parental duties so seriously that he was prepared to marry a socially inferior, penniless, promiscuous little sneak thief to give him the stability he deemed necessary to his wellbeing—never mind the spiteful tittle-tattle that would be bound to surface—couldn't be all bad. So surely, having at least some redeeming features, he would be open to persuasion.

All she had to do was convince him of her integrity. There was nothing she could do about her social or financial status, but she had never stolen a thing in her life—and as for being promiscuous, it was so off the mark it was laughable.

All she had to do was convince him and he would have to respect her as a poor but honest peasant and scrub his crazy idea of trying to persuade her to marry him! That idea had surely been born out of a total lack of respect for her feelings, because being the dregs—in his mind at least—he thought he could make her do whatever suited him.

Marriage would be a disaster. As his wife she would easily find herself believing she was falling in love again—she was silly enough where he was concerned—and her life would be utterly miserable because he had never loved her and never would.

Absorbed in her thoughts, she cannoned straight into him as he waited at the foot of the stairs, his arms going round her in instinctive chivalrous support.

'You smell of heady summer flowers—nice.' His voice was smooth as honey and his arms tightened as his dark head lowered to hers, his taut, proud cheekbones sinking into the soft fall of her silky hair.

With a helpless gasp Sophie felt the length of her body melt with programmed willingness into his. Full breasts peaked urgently against the hard span of his black cashmere covered chest, and the immediate and insistent throbbing between her thighs made her knees go weak, the spicy masculinity of the cologne he used, the underlying unique male scent of him, intoxicating her senses.

He was working his old magic, the potent magic

that made her incapable of reasoned resistance. Helplessly she wriggled closer, heat coiling through her as, unbidden by the mush that passed for her brain, her hands slid up to his broad shoulders and then around his neck, her face lifted expectantly to his.

This was the very last thing she wanted to happen, but how could she deny it? She was as lost as she'd been when he'd walked towards her on that moonlit beach, his face intent on her, drinking in every water-spangled curve and indentation of her near-naked body as he'd scooped up her towel and gently enfolded her—

'Breath back?' Gently he put her away from him. His long mouth curved sardonically. 'Next time look where you're going. I could have been a brick wall. Shall we go?'

The feeling of loss as he stepped away from her was so intense it made her shudder. Lowering her head, so that her hair fell forward to hide a face that was violently daubed with Humiliation Red, Sophie allowed him to tuck a hand beneath her elbow and lead her out to where his car was waiting.

Without any input from her brain she had acted like a sex-mad trollop. She couldn't have made her needs any clearer if she'd been wearing a T-shirt emblazoned with the legend 'I Want To Have Sex With You' across her far too ample chest! And the shaming fact that Ettore hadn't been similarly affected with a similar rush of hormones made her cringe with even more humiliation.

Pushing her aside with a mocking remark about

brick walls when he couldn't have failed to notice how she'd been behaving. Asking for it!

The very real fear that, through sex, he could make her an addict, make her agree to marry him just so she could share his bed whenever he beckoned, was now firmly and finally knocked on the head. She must have been out of her mind when she'd believed that scenario.

He'd house her, feed her and clothe her for the sake of their son. He'd even grit his teeth and marry her for the sake of appearances. But he wouldn't touch the likes of her with a bargepole!

Even more reason to make him believe in her integrity, respect her—a task, she admitted dourly, that was even more difficult after that shameful display.

As the headlights of the powerful car raked through the dusky evening air and they descended to the village Sophie did her utmost to return to being upbeat.

To convince him that she had been wronged. That he'd been acting shamefully when he'd pretended to be madly in love with her just to get her to go to bed with him, all the time knowing he was about to be married to someone else. Force him to see that she wasn't a thief, that she'd been set up. Give him a really guilty conscience and he'd just have to agree to her way out of this mess.

If he continued to flatly refuse to let her set up a home for herself and Torry back in England, then a simple little cottage with a piece of land in this area would do just as well.

He could contribute to Torry's upkeep if he really wanted to, see him at weekends and have him to stay

with him for part of the holidays when he got to
school age. And she would be self-sufficient, grow
all their fruit and vegetables, keep chickens—

'What are you thinking?'

Sophie blinked. His question had startled her.
They were parked in a narrow street outside a stone
building. She hadn't even realised he'd stopped the
car. Still struggling to extricate herself from cosy,
rose-tinted upbeat plans for the future and haul herself back into the far from comfortable present, she
answered without thinking, 'Eggs.'

The sound of his entirely natural rumble of laughter made her tummy curl with pleasure. It had been
such a long, achingly empty time since they'd
laughed together, but she bit down hard on her lower
lip to stop her instinctive answering grin. He wasn't
aware of it, but this evening was going to be serious—deadly serious.

'Hungry, obviously. Good.' Ettore exited the car
at the speed of light, sternly denying the temptation
to put his hands on her shoulders, pull her round to
face him and kiss her until neither of them knew
what day it was.

Back at the house it had taken every last ounce of
his will-power not to take advantage of that melting,
enticing, mind-blowingly sexy little body, pressing
and squirming against his, not to sweep her up in his
arms and into his bed.

He had gone beyond trying to deny the imperative
sexual chemistry that existed between them so he
deserved a medal for forbearance, for seeing a picture
larger than immediate and fantastic self-gratification.
Madonna diavola! He had to get inside her head,

understand what made her what she was, before he could set about her moral reclamation and even think about making love to her, tying her to him as his wife and creating a proper family for his son.

Back in control—well, as much in control as he'd ever be around this little witch—he opened the passenger door and helped her out, carefully keeping physical contact to a minimum as he guided her over the cobbles towards the welcoming lights of the trattoria.

'The food's basic, but superbly cooked. We are early, but later you will be able to meet some of the locals.'

Which was not what Sophie wanted to do—not at this moment in time. She wanted to talk to Ettore, really talk to him, make him see her side of the story.

Ettore was greeted by the rotund proprietor, Beppe, as if he was a valued and favourite relative, while his even more rotund wife beamed from behind a bead curtain that, so far as Sophie could see, led into the kitchen region.

Gaudy hand-painted cupboards flanked an enormous hearth where an untidy log fire flared and fluttered, and Beppe led them over the stone floor to a plain wooden table decorated with a fat candle in a stout terracotta holder.

'Comfortable?' Ettore enquired, his dark eyes level, his smile slight and studiously polite as he moved the candle nearer to the edge of the table, so that there was nothing for her to hide behind.

Was this the way it was going to be? Courteously polite provided she did exactly as she was told? Fell meekly in line with his plans?

'Not very.' She answered his question unhesitatingly, seizing the opportunity to put her oar in and muddy his cold, placid waters, and watched him raise a quizzical brow, leaning back in his seat as Beppe brought a carafe of wine and two glasses to the table.

Alone again, after an animated discussion of vintages, Ettore filled both glasses and levelled at her, 'Why's that, I wonder? You'd have preferred some place glitzy and upmarket?'

Sophie's heart jumped. This was exactly the opening she needed. She took it, her huge grey eyes snapping as she told him forcibly, 'You don't know me at all, do you? Not really.' She lifted one hand, indicating the warm, welcoming and relaxing room, with its quirky cupboards, the herbs hanging from rafters, ancient family photographs in faded velvet frames and dim, sentimental paintings crowded on every inch of wall space. 'This suits me fine. It's down-to-earth, honest—and so am I! I'm not smart or sophisticated—take me to a glittering banquet and I'd spill dinner down my frock!' Her cheeks were burning, peony-pink. She was getting too darn hot, seated so near the fire. Struggling out of her suit jacket, she draped it haphazardly over the back of her seat and got out with a vehemence she couldn't prevent, 'And I'm not a thief and I don't sleep around!'

And I'm a Dutchman! Ettore parried inwardly, but his mouth was quirking at her heated diatribe. She'd be a wow at any function, glittering or otherwise. Utterly gorgeous, eyes like deep pools—sometimes charcoal, sometimes silver—and lips like plump rosebuds, just asking to be kissed. What red-blooded male would be able to keep his eyes, or his hands, for that matter, off those fantastic breasts, temptingly revealed by the ribbed silk cream-coloured sleeveless sweater she was wearing beneath the discarded jacket.

'Don't laugh at me!' she spat like a ruffled kitten as Beppe approached with a chunky earthenware plate of antipasta.

Ettore's lurking smile widened to a grin as he watched the temptation to toss her glass of wine in his face cross her expressive features, an impulse only kept in check, he guessed, by the arrival of olives, tiny vegetable tarts and grilled prawns.

Her dander was up, and this time, instead of being incensed that she should dare to be snippy with him, he found himself enjoying it. Though push her too far and anything might happen! Amazing himself, he found that prospect exhilarating.

With difficulty he straightened his features, but his voice was thickly roughened as he suggested, 'Shall we eat?'

Sophie picked up a plump olive, then put it down again, her heart thumping against her ribs. Unless he got up and walked out she had a captive audience, and she wasn't going to pass up the opportunity.

Folding her arms across her chest, she stated, 'You said we should get to know each other. As I've already told you, you know nothing about me.'

'Right.' Ettore bit into a delicious tartlet. Time to jump in himself, start on that journey he'd promised himself—the journey that would take him inside her head. Time to get serious and stop lusting over her abundant, if superficial physical attributes, pandering to his libido. A libido that had been strangely passive since the night he'd discovered what Sophie Lang really was.

Ettore's sensual mouth flattened. 'Let's start with this. On more that one occasion you've accused me—wrongly, I believe—of ensuring you never worked as a nanny again. I've been wondering why. Because you fell pregnant? Not an even-handed accusation, surely, when you told me you were protected? Which seems to suggest that the larger blame lay with you. Besides, who would employ you as a nanny when you have a small child of your own?'

As a defence, his holier-than-thou attitude stank! Sophie gave him a fulminating glare, selected a prawn and took her time peeling it, her eyes clouding as she remembered what had happened. Her voice held bite as she informed him, 'Immediately after I returned from Italy I was told I'd been sacked from the agency. A serious complaint had been made. By you and that woman you were going to marry—who else? I'd stolen from a guest of my employer. I could expect no references and should think myself lucky that I wasn't being prosecuted.'

Sophie took a long, shuddering intake of breath. It had been a truly terrible time. Ettore had broken her heart, she'd been branded a thief and humiliated. All she'd wanted to do was throw herself back into the career she loved and try to forget she'd ever met him.

'I hadn't stolen anything,' she snapped, her voice brittle with the pain of it all. 'You'd lost me my job and any chance of working in that area again. It really rankled! At the time I didn't know I was pregnant. Luckily there were people who believed in me—unlike you! Nanny Hopkins took me in while I looked for work. A guy took me on at that wine bar, satisfied with a couple of character references—from Nanny Hopkins and my friend Tina's father, who's a GP. So, no thanks to you, I survived!' Her chin came up and the sparky-eyed glare she lanced at him would have shrivelled a lesser man.

She'd peeled a mound of prawns but they lay untouched in a heap amidst the discarded shells, Ettore noted with the part of his mind that wasn't working overtime.

There was no doubt as to the truth of what she was saying. She'd been blacklisted. For the first time since that dreadful night his mind returned willingly to the sombre aftermath. He had been hurting, sick with the betrayal of his love, but he'd insisted on a conference of everyone who knew what had happened: Flavia, Cinzia and Filomena.

His heart beating like a lead pendulum, he'd ordered that the unfortunate episode should go no further. The diamond trinket had been returned; nothing had been lost. Except the dream—more fitting for a green adolescent than an intelligent adult male—of spending the rest of his life with the only woman he had ever loved. Plus a large chunk of his self-respect, he'd added sourly to himself. Even so, he hadn't wanted to see her punished.

Flavia, her eyes moist, had whispered, 'I wouldn't have believed a word of this if you hadn't caught her red-handed. Of course I won't let it go any further.'

Cinzia, a small smile on her scarlet lips, had said nothing. It had been left to Filomena to raise the obvious.

'Shouldn't the agency she works through be informed? She might steal from future employers.'

He had wondered how to make them understand—without sounding like a total wimp—that put out of work Sophie might well resort to darker ways of gathering ill-gotten gains—prostitution even. His blood had thundered in his ears at the hateful images his tormented mind threw up, but it had been Cinzia who had scotched the idea.

'You heard what Signor Severini said. Not a word of this unpleasant episode will go any further. I forbid you to speak of it again.'

His sister Flavia wouldn't have contacted the agency, and Filomena would have been too conscious of the consequences to go against the orders of her mistress to do any such thing. Which left Cinzia—Cinzia, who had stated that she had no intention of pressing charges. At the time such magnanimity had seemed out of character, and now he wondered why.

But it was too early to share his suspicions. He hadn't gained a reputation for hard-headed financial dealings by jumping in without gathering all the relevant information.

Leaning back in his seat while Beppe presented them with a dish of baked sea bass, Ettore studied Sophie's set features, her soft mouth set in a stubborn line. She must have had a tough time coping with the unexpected pregnancy, finding work, earning enough to support herself and save for the coming baby.

Dio! Regardless of the way evidence of theft had so clearly pointed, and her telling silence, she'd been carrying his child and he hadn't given her any support. So he'd been bitter at that time, but that was no excuse! He should have had someone check up on her movements on her return to England. That way he would eventually have learned of the pregnancy! Offered practical help, insisted she return to Italy with him, ensured she had the best possible care while they waited for the birth.

To her credit, she hadn't had an abortion—his hot blood ran cold at the very thought. She had struggled on, alone...

Okay, so he didn't much like himself right now, but regrets were useless. He battened them down with cool efficiency. The future and how it affected his son was all that mattered. And only by getting to know everything about her could it be guaranteed to run smoothly, with no more unpleasant surprises.

Dividing the fish, he passed her a plate. 'How did you manage? You mentioned a nanny—Hopkins?'

Sophie nodded, her mouth still signalling mutiny. She picked up her fork and wished she could attack him with the sharp-pronged instrument instead of the fish! The too-handsome, too-wealthy, too-darned-confident creature had just ignored what she'd said about his having her blacklisted! As if it didn't matter!

She wasn't a violent person, but Ettore Severini brought out the very worst in her. To combat that demeaning trait, she said with ultra-coolness, 'She invited me to share her home and was wonderful. About everything. Always cheerful, seeing silver linings behind every cloud.'

'You had known her a long time?' Ettore topped

up her wine glass. She wasn't eating, but she'd drained her glass as if it had been water. No matter. The alcohol might loosen her tongue.

With a sigh, Sophie lowered her fork and the untasted morsel of fish. It would be a relief to get off the subject of her supposed theft—he obviously found it beneath his dignity to even mention his part in blowing the whistle, never mind look even slightly ashamed for having done so. Because nothing would convince him she hadn't helped herself to that vile woman's diamonds. A relief to talk about someone who had always believed the best of her.

'She was engaged after I was born. My mother had always been frail, apparently. She died when I was three, so I have no clear memory of her. I think Dad always blamed himself for getting her pregnant and me for being born.' She took a swallow of wine to ease her parched throat. It had a subtle hint of strawberries underlying the heady grape, and a fragrance that reminded her of a flower she couldn't quite place. Her mouth curved in a soft smile.

'And?' Ettore prompted, wondering if the refill had been altogether wise. But at least it had got her talking freely.

'Nanny Hopkins was with me until I was seven. Like a mother. Then Dad married Stacia, a divorcee. She had a daughter, Tiffany, and, as she never failed to point out, Tiffany was everything I wasn't. Pretty, graceful, bright.' Her voice wobbled. 'That didn't matter because Nanny Hopkins loved me. Then a few weeks later Stacia dismissed her. Waste of good money, she said—though she didn't mind wasting more than Dad could afford on expensive clothes for her and Tiffany, or caterers for the fancy dinner parties she was always giving.'

She dragged in a long breath, as if regretting having said too much. 'Will you just listen to me?' Her wonderful smile flashed. 'Whining! I had a happy childhood, really. And of course Dad loved me—he just wasn't very good at showing it. Besides, my best friend Tina's family had me to stay with them for school holidays, and we had great times. And Nanny never forgot me. She was always sending letters and little gifts—I was lucky!'

Her smile wavered around the edges and anger tightened Ettore's facial muscles. Lucky? To lose her mother so young? To be made to feel partially responsible for that untimely death? To be brutally deprived of the obviously kindly woman who had taken her place? Not to mention having a stepmother from hell.

He could read between the lines as well as anyone. No expensive clothes for Sophie. Old ones worn until she was bursting out of them? And what young child drew invidious comparisons? Tiffany's supposed superiority in every department must have been rammed down her innocent young throat!

Cool it, he told himself, ignoring the dish of roast vegetables Beppe had slid onto the table as completely as he ignored the impulse to reach across the table and take her small hands in his. This delving was supposed to be forensic, not a haywire mixture of anger, compassion and—and guilt?

'So you moved in with her and worked in a wine bar,' he stated smoothly. 'And Torry was born. Then what?'

Any minute now he was going to lash out at her for what he saw as her irresponsibility in not letting him know he was a father. She could see it coming! But she'd already explained about not wanting to upset the apple cart. She'd thought he'd married that vile woman!

She shrugged. She was beginning to get a thumping headache. And she was sure she wasn't thinking straight, because this was more like an inquisition than a concise statement of her innocence. And why he was interested in where she'd lived, how she'd earned a living of sorts, when he should be concentrating on making a huge apology for his own behaviour, she couldn't imagine. Too much wine. Shouldn't have touched it!

Her tongue felt thick, but she spoke out, aiming to close the subject and get on to what really mattered. 'I got a part-time job at the supermarket round the corner. We managed okay. Then—then she died. It was sudden. The house was rented. Torry and I had to go—' Her voice dried up and her eyes filled with tears. 'I miss her.'

Dio! He saw it all now. Understood why she'd moved in with that blond guy. Without thinking, his mind absorbed with just how she must have felt—grieving for her old friend, suddenly homeless, hopeless, with a young child to care for—he ground out, 'So you moved in with a boyfriend?'

About to add that he perfectly understood why she had taken that step, he found the words forced back, bunching like a lump of solid rock in his chest, as her tearful face iced over and she pushed back her chair and tottered with more haste than dignity across the floor and out through the door.

CHAPTER EIGHT

DROPPING enough euros to cover the cost of their meal plus a generous tip down on the table, Ettore swiftly gathered up Sophie's abandoned jacket and followed, giving himself a mental kick. He hated to see her so hurt. Hated it! His own fault entirely for blurting out like that.

Long strides propelled him over the cobbles. Sophie was leaning against the car, the picture of dejection, head downbent. Gently he draped her jacket over her slender shoulders, opened the passenger door and murmured, 'In you get. The spring nights are cold.'

Obeying—because what other option did she have?—she slumped in her seat, her eyelids drifting down in abject misery as he closed the door at her side and walked round the car to settle himself behind the wheel.

This evening had been a total, utter disaster. She'd intended to convince him once and for all that she was innocent of all charges against her, but he'd discounted whatever she'd managed to say, as if comment of any kind was beneath him, staunchly believing he'd been right to immediately contact the agency she worked through to get her blacklisted because he was certain, beyond any possible doubt, that she was the low sort of creature who would stoop to stealing from a guest in his sister's home.

What earthly hope did she have of making him believe something he didn't want to believe? Why waste her breath in trying?

She felt his head turn towards her and kept her eyes firmly closed. But when he said, 'I'm sorry. I didn't mean to sound censorious about your moving in with that guy,' she batted them open.

Alcohol-fuelled anger stiffened her spine at that patronising excuse for an apology. He had a low opinion of her and he was sticking to it, marking her down as the type of woman who would live off a man in return for sexual favours. Was that why he believed she would jump at his offer of marriage?

Her hands twisted together in her lap as she stared ahead into the dark, starlit Tuscan night. Her words slightly slurred, she came right back. 'Why should you? Sound censorious, I mean. You of all people must understand what it's like to grab what's on offer—you're damn good at it, as I remember!'

'Meaning?' His voice was quiet, level and deadly.

'You really need me to spell it out?' Unfazed by the coldly simmering silence now coming from the driver's seat, Sophie let her voice drip with scorn. 'You think everyone's like you! See something tempting, something easy, and you take it!'

'You are now accusing me of stealing other people's property?' Ettore answered her statement with a quellingly dry bite.

'Worse. You steal hearts—and then—then stamp on them!'

The moment the words were out Sophie was utterly appalled. Fingertips flew to her overheated aching forehead.

He'd know now—wouldn't he just? Know she'd meant it when she'd said she loved him, that she hadn't been playing his game of Casual Holiday Fling! That her silly girlish heart had been well and truly mangled.

Add that to the way her stupid body had so recently and obviously responded to his touch—his merest look!—and he'd know she was still hopelessly in love with him, a real pushover. Know he could twist her round his smallest finger, make her agree to marry him—anything at all as long as she could be with him—and she would never be able to escape him and make a peaceful life for herself and Torry at a safe distance!

Cursing herself for swilling the wine that had led to her telling indiscretion, she cried thinly, 'Take me back!' And wished she'd never been born as she registered the final humiliation, the unstoppable flow of scalding tears that flooded her eyes, soaked her cheeks and dripped off the end of her chin.

His lean face taut, Ettore fired the ignition and pulled away from the cobbled forecourt, all his suspicions reinforced. He glanced at Sophie with narrowed eyes. Frowning darkly, he depressed the accelerator and headed for the hills at speed.

He hated to see her cry! It tore him apart. He and Cinzia between them had done her a terrible wrong. Cinzia actively. He passively.

He had been shocked and savagely hurt by the evidence presented to him, by Sophie's seemingly guilty silence, but now he was sure it had stemmed from a shock as great as his had been.

But that was no excuse! *Madonna diavola*—he should be shot!

When he thought of what she must have gone through he wanted to punch holes in stone walls. Leaving Flavia's home under a terrible cloud, and then, thanks to Cinzia—who else?—being brutally thrown out of work. Later discovering she was pregnant with his child and being unable to come to him for help because she believed he was a recently married man. A lesser woman would have approached him anyway, demanding support, careless of the size of the spanner she threw in the works!

Instead she had coped bravely on her own, bringing their son up in humble circumstances until fate had dealt her another terrible blow with the death of her old friend. So she'd moved in with that blond guy? So what?

So it gave him a sourness in his stomach. But looked at dispassionately, from her viewpoint, what else was the poor kid to do? Suddenly homeless, and out of work because of the death of her old nanny, who'd cared for their beautiful son while she scraped a living at some menial job, she wouldn't have had a wide choice of options—not with a baby to care for. So what right had he to mentally name her *putana*?

Amends would have to be made.

Tomorrow he would take his suspicions—now burning holes in his brain—and confront Cinzia, get the truth out of her. Then he would do what he could to redress his appalling behaviour.

A muffled sob at his side brought his head jerking round. *Dio!* Sitting rigidly to attention, Sophie had her knuckles tightly pressed against her mouth—the classic gesture of someone scared witless.

He immediately slowed to what he considered a snail's pace. He knew these narrow hill roads like the back of his hand, but she didn't. He knew he never took risks, but she didn't. His heart contracted. He'd just earned himself another black mark to add to all the rest! He couldn't wait to get the whole mess sorted out. Get his facts straight. At no level would he consider acting without having everything cut and dried, at his fingertips. And only then would he feel free to move heaven and earth to try to make amends.

'We are almost home,' he assured her gently, taking the final tight bend at a commendable creeping crawl and progressing up the long drive at a hearse-like pace. But if he'd hoped to impress her with his consideration he wasn't doing too well, he recognised, as another muffled sob made him loathe himself.

Home? If only! Sophie swallowed another sob, despising her weakness. This lovely house, set in the beautiful Tuscan countryside, would never be her home—unless she agreed to his cold-hearted offer of marriage.

Yet, still loving him, as she now had to bitterly acknowledge that she did, how could she in all sanity accept such a life sentence? Unfortunately, by refusing to lay herself open to a lifetime of hurts, humiliations and hopeless yearnings, she would be depriving her precious child of everything the son of a Severini could expect. The very best of everything. It was a dilemma that was sending her hysterical!

As the car pulled to a sedate halt in front of the

main door Sophie scrambled out. She tried to steady her wobbling legs by taking a deep breath and telling herself that money and privilege wasn't everything.

'Let me help you.' The kindness of his tone made her want to start crying again, and the supportive arm he slipped around her waist made her want to turn to him, bury her head against the warmth and strength of his broad chest and sob out all her misery.

Telling herself she was made of sterner stuff, Sophie clamped her jaws together and concentrated on walking in a relatively straight line as they approached the main door. Desperately she tried to ignore the warmth of his arm as he held her, the strength of the hand that was pressed to the side of her tiny waist, and didn't really succeed because her heart was thumping like a steamhammer and something wicked was unfurling right at the heart of her.

The door opened easily under his hand and they were in the warmly lit main hall. Sophie had the presence of mind to mumble, 'Thanks. I can manage.'

He obviously didn't think much of that declaration, and Sophie found herself swept up into his arms and carried swiftly up the broad staircase, her heart pattering like crazy as she drank in the fascinating and familiar scent of him, the potent power of his shattering masculinity.

By the time he thrust open the door to her room she was melting all over, Sophie registered with a not entirely unpleasant shock. Dazedly she wondered if he was receiving the messages sent by arms that had somehow wound lovingly around his neck, by a body that was positively snuggling into his, and how she would be able to resist if he decided to act on the information he was receiving.

Her breath shortening, the whole of her body on fire, it took a few moments for her fuddled brain to process the information that her resistance, or probable lack of it, was not about to be tested.

Sliding her down to her feet, Ettore took a smart backward pace, his voice tight and dismissive as he advised, 'Take a shower. As you barely ate a thing, and drank rather too much wine, I will ask someone to bring sandwiches and black coffee.' And he left, closing the door firmly behind him, leaving her to mentally castigate herself for entertaining the ridiculous thought that he still felt any of the old sexual magic that had drawn them together back on the island.

That he had never loved her was in no doubt. Lying about eternal devotion was the oldest trick in the book, aimed to ensure she returned willingly to his bed time after eager time.

But now he didn't even desire her.

A sobering thought. And one she shouldn't need reminding of after plenty of past evidence.

Summoning all her reserves of common sense, she tartly told herself to hold onto that thought and never let herself forget it again—because it strengthened her conviction that marriage was completely out of the question.

A cold shower enabled her to regain the senses that had gone missing when she'd been held so close in his arms.

Slipping into one of the filmy silk nightdresses she had acquired during her travels through Europe, she wrapped her hair in a turban-tied towel, then tossed it aside impatiently. Her hair could dry on its own.

Out of the *en suite* bathroom, she registered that someone had deposited a tray of coffee and a plate bearing a couple of small crusty rolls stuffed with a variety of fillings on the low table next to the comfy brocade-covered armchair to one side of the massive bed.

Her stomach lurched. Hot coffee she could handle—but food?

'Eat.'

Ettore's voice startled her, bringing her head round. He stood near the door, in shadows not touched by the soft glow from the shaded lamp next to the bed. Covered by confusion, her hard-won composure flying out through the walls, Sophie could only stare. Drink in that impressive physique, the hard planes of his devastating features, the glint of those dark eyes that seemed welded to hers. Her own eyes misted with the sting of more despised tears.

If she wept again, he would be lost. Ettore knew it, and struggled to regain the resolve that earlier had allowed him to set her down on her feet and walk away with honour, when every atom of his being had been crying out for the ecstatically intimate melding of his hard boy to the soft, yielding femininity of hers.

Watching her, watching the warm colour flood her lovely face, the glow from the lamp caress the enticingly lush contours tantalisingly glimpsed through the thin, lovingly clinging silk of the ivory-coloured nightdress she was wearing, he felt his body harden. That she wasn't immune to him made her even more tempting. His throat thickened. *Dio!* Didn't he have any integrity? Until his suspicions were confirmed Sophie was strictly off limits, and even then the air would have to be cleared before their relationship—if they were ever to have something truly worthwhile—could move forward.

His chest expanded on a harsh, painfully indrawn breath. She might physically respond to him—a hormone thing—but the perfect gift of her love was no longer his. After his less than understanding treatment of her since he'd found her in London she would hate him. And he couldn't blame her.

She moved. Just a little. Edging nearer to the support of the armchair. Silky fabric moved with her body, clinging to the shape of her thighs, to the slight feminine curve of her tummy.

Ettore began to sweat.

He shouldn't be here. With her like this. It was more than flesh and blood could stand! Unconsciously, his hands fisted.

What had possessed him to prepare the tray himself? His self-righteous excuse had been a disinclination to disturb the staff he had given leave to take the evening off. But all the time what he'd really wanted was to be with her, make sure she wasn't still upset. Look at her, touch her. Want to be with her…

He moved. Helplessly drawn towards her. Glistening silver-grey eyes lifted to his. Shallow breathing. Dark eyes lowered to the rapid rise and fall of her chest, her beautiful breasts straining against the sheer cradling silk.

His throat thickened. His heart hammered.

'Sophie?'

Was that a question? Was this him? Was this the self-confident alpha male who up until this moment had inhabited the skin of Ettore Severini? Or was he now a humble supplicant, a worshipper at the feet of an angel, struck low and inarticulate beneath the force of what he was feeling for this woman?

Her lush lips parted, trembled, as if she were seeking to make some kind of response. Her small bare feet shifted on the thick carpet. His awareness of her, of how he craved her, shook him to the depths of his being, and as suddenly as it had been stripped from him the power was back.

A touch was all it took. Just one. Just the palm of his hand on the satin-smooth skin of a warm naked shoulder. And then he was reaching for her.

With a tiny gasp she came willingly, melting against him as his hands curved round the enticing flare of her hips and pulled her into the hard ache of his manhood.

All thoughts of resistance, of self-preservation, and every scrap of pride disappeared in the flicker of an eyelash as his mouth invaded hers. He did desire her! For some reason his past actions, his seeming indifference, had appeared to deny it, but now the walls were down. The old magic was back with a vengeance, a force stronger than both of them combined.

Blind emotion claimed her as her mouth answered his raw passion. Greedy fingers curved into the luxurious thickness of his dark-as-night silky hair as the heat of his arousal, hard against the yielding softness of her tummy, turned her into a delirious wreck.

He tore his mouth from hers, only to bury it in the

deep cleft between her swollen and unbearably sensitised breasts, and Sophie's pulses leapt with electrifying sensation. Her head flung back as long fingers pushed down the narrow straps, peeling the fabric from the twin pink-tipped engorged globes.

Another swift movement and her nightdress pooled at her feet. With a smothered, wickedly sexy groan Ettore held her slightly away from him, his hooded eyes magnetic, holding her in thrall, as they very thoroughly slid like a caress over her unashamed nakedness.

'I burn for you, my Sophie,' he breathed on a driven undertone. 'Come to me.'

The part of her brain that would have had her telling him to get lost, that she had no intention of being conned a second time, had closed down. No one at home. The veiling of her starry eyes with the sweep of thick lashes and the smallest dip of her blonde head was drugged acquiescence—all he needed to enclose his arms around her and carry her to the waiting bed.

He stood above her, his tanned fingers intent on hauling the black cashmere sweater off his magnificent torso, and Sophie could only stare and quiver with the fierce heat of desire as her needy eyes rediscovered every all-male inch of the body she had once known better than her own.

He had lied to her, deceived her, treated her as if she were contaminated. But she was his woman. She had borne his child. He would never know it, but she would love him always, warts and all. This one last night with him would be all she would ever have or ask for. More than that—marriage, even rights over her body on a casual basis—would destroy her.

That for him this would be a natural slaking of the lust of a highly sexed male animal was something she wasn't about to start worrying about.

She was his woman. And this just had to be fate. That was her last coherent thought as he lowered his superb naked length beside her. And reached for her.

CHAPTER NINE

SOPHIE stirred. Thick, blonde-tipped lashes lifted just enough to tell her that early sunlight was streaming through the partly open louvres. She smiled blissfully, eyelids drifting closed again, a surge of almost uncontainable joy making her body glow as she reached for him.

Empty space where he had lain when they'd finally fallen asleep, wrapped closely in each other's arms.

A sharp stab of frightening insecurity was quickly stamped on. She would not go there! Never again would she torment herself by looking for dark motives, Sophie vowed staunchly as she stretched her sated body with luxurious abandon.

So he'd woken early, slipped back to his own room, gone out for a walk, gone fishing—so what? It didn't signify anything. She might be his mistress, sort of—as of last night—and if he still wanted it she would soon be his wife, but she wasn't his keeper. He didn't have to clear every move he made with her before he made it.

Last night had altered everything. She had to give what they did have a chance and stop thinking of the downside. And not just for Torry's sake either, but for her own—loving him, how could she be whole and happy without him?—and for Ettore's sake, too.

He needed his son, needed to know his child was happy and beautifully cared for, had all the advantages he could give him. They could marry and be happy. A happy family. The three of them. It might

take her considerable time and the expenditure of a
great deal of patient forbearance to get him to believe
she wasn't what he thought she was—the evidence
against her was stacked high; she had to admit that—
but she'd get there in the end.

Last night had shown her that it could be done.
Their lovemaking had been so wildly emotional at
first. It hadn't been just about sex, because if it had
been she would have known it and woken this morning feeling besmirched, hating herself, instead of
feeling gloriously confident in the future they could
have together.

It had been as if two eager souls had found each
other again after being lost in dark limbo, clinging
to each other, almost sobbing with raw passion. The
second time it had transcended mere ecstasy. Slow,
tenderly explorative, divinely special, two souls
home, dissolving into each other.

So even if his head told him she was a worthless
little tramp, his body and maybe even his heart already told another story. On a basic physical level
he needed her just as much as she needed him, and
with love on her side and his eventual and necessary
recognition of her innocence they would stay the distance.

Her breathy sigh of pleasure at the rightness of her
newly found confidence was swallowed as a knock
on the door heralded the arrival of the housekeeper
with a large cup of coffee on a silver tray.

'It is the good morning,' she announced in her
careful English, and Sophie beamed and hauled herself up against the pillows, clutching the sheet over
her naked breasts. 'Spring has come to stay with us.'
She placed the tray on the bedside table, diplomati-
cally disregarding the rumpled silky nightdress so
unceremoniously dropped the night before. 'Signor

Severini left half an hour ago and asked me to tell you that he has business in Firenze for one, maybe two days. As the morning is so good I will bring breakfast to you out in the courtyard. Yes?'

'Thank you.' It was as much as Sophie could do to get the pleasantry out, to smile and reach over to cradle the coffee cup in suddenly unsteady hands. Despite her good intentions doubts flooded back. She hated them, but they insisted on creeping in, spoiling things.

Why hadn't he woken her to say goodbye, explain where he was going and why, instead of leaving a message with his housekeeper? It would only have taken a moment or two out of his busy day. Didn't she rate that much consideration? Had she seen what she wanted to see last night instead of what was really there?

Hold it there! she grouched at herself as the housekeeper left the room. Just stop it! She was asking too much of him, too soon. He had already committed to their son, and to her as his son's mother because she was needed by Torry. It would take a lot longer for him to commit to her as a person in her own right, to her as a wife who was much more than an extra piece of luggage, dragged about because she was needed on the journey of their son's life.

But she had time on her side. That was her sensible thought as she finished her coffee and slid out of bed. It was a beautiful day and she was early enough to bath and dress Torry. The three of them could breakfast together in the courtyard, where the fountain played and tubs of narcissi perfumed the air—Minette would like that—and when Torry took his afternoon nap she could continue her now-and-then Italian lessons with the housekeeper—because if she was going to make her life here she would need to speak as fluently as the natives.

As Ettore drove out of Florence his heart kicked in his chest. It had been just as he'd begun to strongly suspect. Cornered, Cinzia had told him all he needed to know. Sophie had been set up, just as she'd so often protested.

And he hadn't listened! Faced with the 'evidence' he'd been shattered. His long-standing friendship and respect for Cinzia had taken precedence over anything else, and he hadn't listened. He had been fond of Cinzia—he'd never loved her, but had trusted and respected her. He would never in a million years have believed her capable of such duplicity.

Cursing his closed mind, the initial shock and deep hurt that had self-protectively turned into the stiff-necked pride that had allowed him to believe the worst of his wronged Sophie, he stood on the accelerator. He needed to be with her, to start trying to put things right.

Would Sophie give him a second chance? She might have enjoyed making love with him, but could she ever fall in love with him again after the way he had behaved?

Despite the car's efficient air-conditioning system he began to sweat and, realising he might be stopped by the traffic cops, causing further unendurable delay, he slowed down and tried to fix his mind on something other than his gorgeous, wronged Sophie.

Suspicions, having taken root when it had become obvious that someone had gone against his instruction that the theft should not be reported back to the agency, had grown into certainty. But he'd needed to check. He worked with facts, always had, not on assumptions. And early this morning he'd set out to find them. He had the clout.

Calling in a favour that had given him access to confidential material, he'd verified those suspicions.

On the day of Flavia's ill-fated birthday party Cinzia's father had already been in worrying financial difficulties, so—as she had this lunchtime savagely verified—when he'd taken her aside to gently break the news that their marriage of convenience wouldn't happen, because he'd finally and deeply fallen in love with Sophie, Cinzia had known she had to do something drastic to keep her future marriage to a bottomless money pot on track.

Instructing Filomena to plant the diamond choker in Sophie's luggage and making the subsequent 'discovery' had done the trick. It had been pure spite that had led her to contact the agency. The way she had for the very first time pressed for the actual marriage to take place soon, when up until then she had been as laid-back about taking the plunge as he had been, now made sense.

The di Barsini family were now on the financial rocks. Her earlier denials had been defensive lies. Her father's final ill-advised last throw of the dice—a high-risk investment with borrowed capital—had lost him everything, threatening the imminent public disclosure of bankruptcy. Little wonder Cinzia had finally decided to bite the bullet and press for marriage and an end to their long engagement.

The interview with her today over a lunch neither had eaten had been deeply unpleasant. How he could ever have gone along with the outdated idea of a sterile dynastic marriage with such a creature gave him goosebumps. It might have seemed a sensible tradition at one time, but now it turned his stomach.

Refusing to dwell on the past when the future was

so very important, Ettore swiftly turned his mind to trying to figure out how he could persuade Sophie to forgive him, to try and love him again as she once had done. As he loved her.

The late-afternoon heat was cooling towards a deep amethyst evening as Sophie wandered back to the villa barefoot, over grass studded with fragrant narcissi and the bruised purple buds of wild irises.

Torry was sound asleep in the nursery, tired after another day of new scents and sounds and the exciting discovery that he could almost, with his mother's hands firmly around his round little body, stand on his own two feet.

She would have to change out of the worn old jeans and collarless cambric shirt—of pre-makeover vintage—and make herself respectable. Trig herself up in one of her many elegant little designer dresses for eating her solitary dinner at one end of the vast dining table in the *sala da pranzo* and try to stop willing Ettore to come home. Now. This evening. Not make her wait until tomorrow!

Home to her.

Her stomach flipped, just as if she'd been in a lift that had whooshed her skywards at supersonic speed and dropped her back to earth just as swiftly. She wanted him so badly it made her breathless and giddy just thinking of him and what they could, in time, have together—provided she had the faith and forbearance to change his opinion of her morals.

Reaching the cool interior of the great hall, she paused to let her breathing return to normal. She was wondering if she would ever manage it, when her body still sang from last night's passion, when the housekeeper emerged from the now gathering shadows that led to the staff quarters.

'You had a phone call, *signorina*. English man. The name Tim. You are to contact him. There is some urgency, I think. You have his number? I didn't think to ask.'

'Yes, of course. I'll phone from my room.' A smile. No hint of the sudden sweep of guilt that made her feel really awful. She'd phoned, as promised, on her arrival here, but not since, and she'd said she would. She'd had too much on her mind to remember her promise.

Her room felt over-warm and airless. She left the door open and flung open the windows, gratefully breathing in the cooler breeze before hunting in her purse for the card Tim had given her all that time ago. Clutching it, she sank down on the bed, curled her legs beneath her and punched in his number.

'You okay?' he asked gruffly, as soon as she gave her name. 'I haven't heard a dicky-bird since the day you arrived. You promised to phone again in a couple of days. For all I knew he could have locked you away and lost the key. And Tina's going spare. She blames me for letting that guy drag you and the kid away. Is he treating you okay? From what I saw of him when he collected you and your stuff he looked pretty formidable.'

'We're just fine, and Ettore dotes on Torry. He even—' her face went pink with sheer happiness '—wants me to marry him, and I'm going to tell him I will,' Sophie assured him, her soft mouth curving. 'So tell Tina not to worry. I'll phone her myself and put her mind at rest. I'm sorry,' she breathed, guilt striking again. 'I should have got round to contacting you both before now.'

'So you should be sorry!' Tim came back, trying to sound stern and big-brotherly and failing. 'I'm glad things are working out, if that's what you want, but the olds and Tina have been giving me a hard time. I should have been looking after you and the kid, and they hold me personally responsible for letting some strange guy as good as abduct you!'

Swallowing a giggle—it wasn't funny, and it was good to know that there were people who really cared enough to worry about her, and she hated to think that Tim had been put through the wringer—Sophie said contritely, 'Don't feel like that, Tim. He is my baby's father—what else could I have done in the circumstances? I'll make it right for you, I promise.'

A movement in the open doorway caught her peripheral vision and she swung around, the receiver clamped to her ear, her huge eyes suddenly glitteringly bright.

Ettore! Home at last! She wasn't going to have to endure another night and day before she saw him again!

An ecstatic smile on her face, she turned back to the phone and quickly, quietly, ended the call, promising to contact Tina and rapidly jotting down her old friend's Canadian number before turning back to the man who was the one and only, the love of her life.

But empty space greeted her.

Considerately leaving her in peace to finish her phone call, he'd probably gone to look in on his sleeping son. She'd go and find him and this evening—maybe after dinner, maybe out on the terrace in the moonlight, because she wanted the occasion to be special—she would tell him she would marry him.

She felt indescribably happy. Everything, eventually, would be all right. She just knew it. They were in for the long haul, a lifetime together—plenty of time to convince him she wasn't a thieving little slapper! She was sure, after his tenderness last night, she was already on the way to achieving it.

She was deliberating over whether to change swiftly out of her old grunge and get into one of the exquisite dresses he had provided her with and make herself look a bit more attractive, or to run and find him, like right at this moment, when the phone rang.

After only a moment's hesitation she snatched it up and gave the number in muddled Italian, her breath catching when her *bête noir* said with sugary venom, 'Cinzia di Barsini here. I just wondered if you're proud of yourself. Right now I imagine you are. It is what you would call a red letter day for you, yes? By using the oldest trick in the book you've managed to break up an engaged couple who were made for each other.'

Sickened by the poisonous tone of the woman she just knew had set her up all that time ago, Sophie was tempted to replace the receiver. But the news that Ettore hadn't been the free man she'd imagined him to be, had actually still been engaged to marry the other woman, had left her bed this morning to drive to Florence to break the engagement off and confess he'd asked his son's mother to marry him, left her stunned into keeping her ear glued to the phone in shattered, sickly, perverse fascination.

'But don't be too pleased with yourself,' the hated voice purred. 'He's only marrying you for the kid's sake—he's got more honour than you could ever dream of. You've trapped him, and he hates that. And he'll end up hating you for it. When we said our goodbyes today he looked as if he already did. I've never seen the poor darling look so hopeless. It's me he's always wanted to marry. And he's ashamed of you—well, who wouldn't be? He won't be faithful—or haven't you figured that out yet? He'll play away. A common little thing like you hasn't got what it takes to satisfy such a highly sexed sophisticated man. The people in our circle won't even pity you—they'll simply laugh at you—'

Sophie slid the receiver home with shaking fingers. Everything that vile woman had said was poisonously hateful.

But sickeningly true.

CHAPTER TEN

ETTORE knotted the plain dark blue tie that added the final sober touch to his charcoal shirt and narrow-fitting black trousers. The reflection that stared back at him from the pier glass was unrelievedly sombre. He looked as if he were about to attend a funeral. That was his painfully wry thought as he went down to dinner.

The funeral of his hopes.

He had never felt less like eating, but the motions had to be gone through. Italians might be famed for their volatile natures, but Severinis never wore their hearts on their sleeves. Hurts must be kept inside. Appearances were to be maintained.

Tonight he had to offer her her freedom.

While he lived he would never forget the moment when every last one of his hopes had died. Not screaming and fighting, but with the dark still silence of helpless inevitability.

His heart had been swollen with love for his enchanting Sophie, the mother of his son, pounding with excited anticipation, with the intoxicating memory of her passion and sweetness of the night before, and he'd gone to her room to begin the process of making amends, of persuading her that he could be worthy of her love.

She'd been curled up on her bed—the scene of the sheer ecstasy he had only ever found with her, of so much wonder. In his absence she'd reverted to the type of clothes she was obviously comfortable with, disdaining designer labels. She'd been speaking to the guy she had moved in with before he'd forced her to leave him.

His already stricken conscience had been left writhing in mortal agony as he'd heard her heartfelt, 'Don't feel like that, Tim. He is my baby's father—what else could I have done in the circumstances? I'll make it right for you, I promise.'

How she aimed to do that propelled a spear of agonising jealousy straight into his heart. But that wasn't the issue. The only issue was the way he had behaved.

He'd had no right to make demands. The circumstances she'd talked about had given her no option but to do as he said. He'd had no right to drag her away from her country, her friends, the man she had moved in with—the man she loved? No right to try to stamp her with his own standards—expensive designer gear, top-of-the-range accessories and make-up—turning her into his idea of how the mother of his son should present herself. And he'd thought the very worst of her, dismissing her protestations of innocence as so much bluster. Even when he'd started to have his suspicions about Cinzia, in his arrogance he hadn't shared them with her.

He'd been piling wrong on unforgivable wrong.

She was already in the dining room. His face set—he refused to let his pain show in his eyes—he greeted her coolly, took his place opposite her, at the far end of a table that could comfortably seat twenty, and shook out his napkin.

Tonight she looked heartbreakingly beautiful. All flags flying. Because she knew it was expected of her? Gone were the comfortable old casuals she would have worn from choice. Dressed now in Milan's finest. Something in silky material in a soft amethyst shade that deepened the colour of her clear grey eyes, left her arms bare and dipped discreetly between those magnificent breasts.

Smartly he diverted his attention to the food that had just been served to him, ignoring the wine. His tongue would not be loosened. By his behaviour, his crass mistrust, he had forfeited any right to speak of his love, to beg for a second chance.

Sophie chewed something she couldn't for the life of her swallow because her throat had closed up. Ettore looked so austere, his strikingly handsome, lean, dark features forbidding. The sombreness of the clothes he was wearing seemed very fitting, perfect for the doomy occasion.

And for that she had to be thankful, she supposed, as tears pricked behind her eyes. If he'd shown the slightest, the very slightest hint that he remembered what they'd shared last night—valued it as something blissfully special—the tiniest hint of warmth, she would have been completely undone, unable to get through what she knew had to come next.

After she'd put the phone down on Cinzia she'd been in a state of shock, all thoughts of finding Ettore vanished. Sitting on the edge of the bed, she'd gradually pulled her tumultuous thoughts into some kind of order.

Ettore was nuts about his son, so he'd gritted his teeth and offered to marry her to legitimise their child. She'd said no. The part of him that craved his high status, beautiful and wealthy fiancée would have been relieved, even though duty told him otherwise.

This morning he must have woken up to horror. He'd betrayed the woman he really wanted as his wife not once, but twice. He'd fled to her side, his sense of honour making him confess, end the engagement, because he had a duty to his son and his son's mother had welcomed him to her bed with huge hunger. It looked like she had changed her mind about marriage.

No wonder he looked as if the light had gone out on his life, Sophie agonised as she took a huge swig of wine to help the obstruction in her mouth down her throat. And it was mostly her fault. Somehow she was going to have to make it right.

As her plate was taken away and another put in its place she leant back in her chair. She couldn't even look at what had been served, much less make another abortive attempt to eat.

Quietly dismissing the maid, Ettore rose to his feet. Six foot plus of sexual dynamite.

'As neither of us appears to be hungry, I suggest we take coffee outside.'

Bereft of speech, Sophie stumbled to her feet, her stomach going into freefall, then recovering itself somewhere back around her throat.

Crunch time. And she would just have to bear it. Because she loved him far more than her life and she wanted him to be happy.

Needed to know he was happy, living the charmed life he and Cinzia had mapped out for themselves, not a life forced on him.

She had to lie as she'd never lied before in the whole of her life. Tell him that last night had meant nothing. She still wouldn't marry him. Swear that she and Torry would melt discreetly away, that he could see the little boy whenever he felt he wanted to, and urge him to assure Cinzia that she, Sophie, would never intrude or make demands of any kind—would be unheard, invisible. If the other woman had been as gutted by the ending of her engagement as she had sounded she could surely be persuaded to over-look his infidelity, regard it as a meaningless fling that would never be repeated.

Coffee was waiting for them. Set out on the table where, this morning, she, Torry and Minette had breakfasted in sunlight. She had been so happy then.

'Won't you sit?'

A lump the size of a house in her throat now, Sophie sat in the chair he was holding out for her with chilling politeness. He had spoken to her, but she knew from the cool distance of his voice, the rigid line of his powerful shoulders, that he had shut her out.

He would be feeling pretty disgusted with himself. Giving in to base animal lust wasn't exactly an ad-mirable trait, one that he could be proud of, but her mistake—forgetting to take her contraceptive pill which, scattily, she'd thought she was only taking to regulate her periods—had meant that he was now looking at a very different future with a very different woman than the one he'd hoped for.

'Are you cold?' The slender hand that lifted the chased silver coffee pot was shaking, Ettore noted with aching sympathy as he sat opposite her. Well out of touching distance. He wasn't sure he could resist reaching out for her if they were closer.

'I'm fine.' She passed his cup, pushing it over the surface of the table. To her own mortification she knew she'd sounded as if she were being strangled. In the dusky light, silvered by starshine, his features were bleak. He looked exactly what he was: a man who had committed himself to stern duty. She could put it off no longer. She had to set him free to be with the woman who'd vowed they were meant for each other. She loved him so and couldn't bear to think she had ruined his life.

She took a shaky breath, willing her heavily beating heart to slow down, her mouth to stop wobbling. Until those two feats were accomplished she wouldn't be able to say her piece and sound determined and practical, glad to cut all ties with him save those of a shared child.

'You don't look it.' She looked on the verge of tears. The aftermath of her earlier conversation with the guy she'd wanted to live with? A fraught conversation that had doubtless reminded her of the life she and the Tim guy had planned together? That she'd made love with him last night wasn't something he'd hold against her. He wasn't into double standards.

Throughout his long engagement to Cinzia di Barsini he'd been free to take a mistress, with his fiancée's tacit agreement, because in their circles such arrangements were totally acceptable. It was a freedom he had, until finding Sophie, availed himself of on only a couple of utterly forgettable occasions.

'I won't keep you long,' he imparted heavily. 'Out

here we are guaranteed privacy. Do say if you're cold. I'll fetch a wrap.' All he craved was the liberty to take her in his arms and warm her body with his, to hold her, care for her, treasure her.

She shook her head, and was gearing herself up to say her piece when he knocked the words right out of her head with a taut, 'You are free to leave as soon as you wish to. I was wrong to insist that you left your homeland. You may take Torry and return to England, if that is your wish. Naturally I insist on reasonable access, and I will support him, and you, financially. However—' His long fingers curled round his cup, the knuckles tightening until they showed white beneath the tanned skin. 'I would like to think of you—and my son—living within reach of the open countryside and clean air. I will make the necessary funds available to facilitate such a move.'

'There's no need to buy me off!' Heat returned to Sophie's cold-as-stone body with a fiery rush. So much for her noble intentions of setting him free to be with his wonderful, socially acceptable Cinzia! He had taken matters into his own hands—decided that his broken engagement was too high a price to pay for his son.

Forgetting that until last night she would have given everything to hear the words he'd just spoken, if only to save herself from the pain of living with a man who would never love her, she struggled to get to her feet—but subsided with a thump as he put in swiftly, 'You are owed, Sophie. There's no question of my buying you off.' And then, despising himself utterly for his shaming weakness he added, 'There is another option. My offer of marriage still stands.'

Sophie felt as if her heart had exploded with pain, her face whitening as she struggled for breath. She'd spent most of the day soppy with happiness, convinced they could have a great life together. Convinced that accepting his one-off proposal of marriage was right for both of them. Living in a silly girlie dream. She had believed he was a free man. But he was not.

She lifted her eyes to his and her mouth trembled. He was putting his future in her hands and she had never loved him more.

Say the word and he'd go through with it. His sense of honour would see to that. It had already made him remind her of that second option. It must have taken a great deal of courage to get the words out.

She couldn't and wouldn't do that to him.

Gaining her feet took a monumental effort. Schooling her voice to an even level took even more, as she managed, 'May I leave the arrangements for our flight with you? Bearing in mind I'd like to leave with Torry as soon as possible.'

CHAPTER ELEVEN

SPRING was at last making a tentative appearance in England, but as yet it hadn't made any noticeable impression on the grey London street where Sophie lived with that blond guy.

Lived with her lover, Ettore growled savagely at himself. Just face it!

The house was depressing, just as he remembered it. Borderline seedy. The sooner Sophie and his son moved into something far more salubrious the better.

The lover would go with them?

Probably.

The thought of the other guy being around his son twenty-four-seven when he, his father, would have to make an appointment to see his own flesh and blood made him want to kick holes in brick walls! But it was what Sophie had chosen—what she wanted.

An iron band of tension tightened around his temples as he thrust back his shoulders and mounted the steps.

A fortnight wasn't a suspiciously short length of time, was it? Of course not. Not like him to be unsure of anything. *Inferno!* He had every right to drop by and see his own son! Two weeks was already too long.

Besides, there was the matter of the financial settlement, her signature on the document in his briefcase. Something his lawyers could have handled, but which he preferred to do himself.

Why? Scrub the excuses he'd come up with: the saving of time, personally making sure she understood the legalities. He ached to see her, that was why. Not that it would show. He wouldn't let it.

His mouth hardened as he thrust open the street door.

And it tightened until he felt his jaw might snap in two as the guy—Tim, she'd called him—clattered down the stairs.

'What do you want?' Tim was the first to break the charged silence, the note of belligerence stark in the musty air.

The kid's father, Tim recognised in minor panic. All perfectly groomed, six-foot-plus of expensive Italian tailoring, harsh won't-give-an-inch features. Rich as Croesus, power-mad.

Remembering the endless ear-bashing he'd got from Tina and his parents when he'd let this bastard drag Sophie and her kid away that first time, he was torn. Should he stay around to make sure it didn't happen again, and then be back late from his lunch-break—not a good idea for a new manager on probation?

He fabricated with breathless speed, off the top of his head, 'If you've come to see Sophie, she's out with the kid. They'll be gone all day. I'll take a message. If you want access in the future, you'd better make an appointment.'

He pulled back his thin shoulders, horribly conscious of the Italian's aura of bred-in-the-bone dominance, his obvious physical superiority, and instinctively aware that this man wouldn't stand idly by while he received a mouthful of what he would see as abuse from a mere nobody. He had to force himself to find enough bottle to mumble, 'Why don't you leave her alone? You've done enough damage. She won't say what you did, but you've only got to look at her to know you put her through the wringer. You've hurt her enough already. So stay clear!'

And he scarpered before the killing look in those black eyes could be translated into physical action, congratulating himself that the Italian would now make tracks, believing Sophie was out with the kid.

The other man had been lying, Ettore decided without rancour. Where the shabby old pram had once stood there was now a secondhand-looking buggy. Tim had been protecting his Sophie. Ettore understood the feeling. But protecting her from what?

Sophie had what she wanted, he told himself acidly. She'd had the choice. She'd freely chosen this gangly chap in his off-the-peg blue suit, blond hair gelled in place, with his open, honest face, and this seedy house, over him and the life of luxury he had told her was hers for the taking. He'd asked himself why on too many occasions to count, and had shamingly come up with the same answer every time.

She'd once heatedly told him that Tim had believed in her innocence implicitly, no question. While he had named her thief and liar.

Her choice, though it had hurt like hell and still did, made sense. He, with his pride, arrogance and distrust, had forfeited any right to expect her love.

Just punishment. No arguing with that, he reminded himself heavily.

Unused to and despising such negative thoughts, bordering on self-pity, Ettore took the stairs two at a time. When she'd chosen to return to England he'd been too gutted to do anything other than make the arrangements with icy, silent efficiency. Neglecting to tell her of the suspicions that had now been verified by a cornered Cinzia.

Time to put that right. She might not want to see him, but he owed her that much. An apology. Time to let her know of the generous settlement that would enable her and his son to leave this dump and make a decent life.

Then maybe his conscience would lie easy. Though his heart never would.

Sophie put Torry down in his cot, scarcely daring to breathe, and gently covered him with a soft blanket, mentally crossing her fingers. He did, at long last, look as if he might actually fall asleep. Her back and arms ached from carrying him round all morning and most of the night as she tried to comfort her fractious baby.

The poor little darling was teething again, if the angry red smudge on one cheek was anything to go by. She pushed her mussed hair back off her face, and her eyes momentarily lost their now habitual bruised, punished look, her mouth curving in a smile that for once wasn't forced as she watched him fall asleep.

Coffee was the only thought in her head as she

walked with exaggerated, silent care into the tiny kitchen. Hot, black, and very, very strong.

She'd been up with Torry most of the night, rubbing gel into his poor inflamed gums, rocking him against her shoulder, because whenever she put him down he started to cry again and she didn't want Tim's rest to be disturbed. He'd been so good to them, insisting they stay until she'd got their future sorted out.

Tim, bless him, hadn't turned a hair when she and Torry had landed on his doorstep a fortnight ago. She'd had nowhere else to go.

As she cradled the mug of scalding coffee in both hands and ambled into the sitting room she told herself that things were looking up, even if her heart still wept and told her differently.

In another fortnight's time Tim's parents would be returning from their visit to Tina and their son-in-law in Canada, and they were pressing her to make a home temporarily with them, in their bungalow on the outskirts of a tiny picture-postcard Herefordshire village.

'Basil and I talked it over,' Enid Dunmore had stated only a couple of days ago. 'There's a nice guest room that's rarely used, and you've always been like one of the family—you know that, Sophie dear. It will be healthier for you and baby Torry, and besides, you must make sure the father supports you financially. I gather he's wickedly wealthy. So you shouldn't have to worry about making a living for you and the baby. I don't see why he shouldn't buy a property for you—somewhere near to us, where we can help out with babysitting and generally make

ourselves useful. Being a single parent can't be easy.
So until you can get things sorted out you must stay
with us.'

Curling up on the long leather sofa, Sophie sipped
the hot brew and pondered Enid's suggestion. Short
on family—her stepmother and sister wouldn't shed
a tear if she disappeared off the face of the earth
tomorrow—it would be nice for Torry to have adop-
tive grandparents close by. The Dunmores had always been closer to her than her own dysfunctional
family. But she would like to work again, when
Torry was old enough for nursery school. She wanted
to be independent, and not have to rely on handouts
from Ettore even if she was entitled.

And she hadn't given a thought to Ettore's offer
of financial support. When she thought of him at
all—which, despite all her good intentions, she found
herself doing a trillion times a day—it was to wonder
if his engagement to Cinzia was back on again. If he
was happy, with his life going the way he wanted. If
his high-status woman had decided to overlook his
fall from grace—bedding someone no better than a
peasant—and whether he'd passed on the message
that she, Sophie, wouldn't make waves, would stay
well out of their lives.

When the doorbell rang—long, loud and insistent—she stumbled groggily to her feet, fighting to
keep her leaden eyelids open. The slightest sound
could wake Torry, and the poor little poppet needed
his sleep.

Tim. It had to be. Forgotten something? Forgotten
his door key, too, by the sound of it! He'd taken to
coming back at lunchtime for a sandwich, instead of

piling into the burger bar across the road from where he worked. Checking she was okay, he said. Even though she'd told him she was fine. He'd be late back now...

Flinging the door open, prepared for Tim to rush past her, all gangly legs and arms, and retrieve whatever he'd forgotten, she found herself staring up into that beloved, starkly handsome, starkly unsmiling face. Her clucky smile vanished.

For a moment she held his suddenly frowning gaze and then her stricken eyes fell. So soon. She hadn't expected this. Didn't know if she could handle it.

'If you've come to see Torry—I'm afraid he's asleep,' she gabbled thinly, clutching at the edge of the door as if to bar his entrance. She wanted to see him so badly it frightened her. And she wanted him to disappear, to save her the savage pain of being within touching distance, and that frightened her too, because she wanted to keep him with her always and that couldn't happen.

She wasn't yet strong enough to deal with this, she thought in acute misery as he strode past her into the centre of the room and laid his briefcase on the low coffee table, nudging aside her half-empty coffee mug and last night's newspaper.

'Then I will see him when he wakes.' His mouth was taut. *Inferno!* What had happened to her? Her face was all huge bruised eyes, pale, trembling mouth, and the defeated droop of her head on the slender stalk of her neck gave her the look of a woman who'd been put through hell.

Down to him, so her lover had accused. Nonsense!

She'd chosen freely to return to this dreary place, to live with her callow lover.

A sudden thought turned the blood in his veins to ice. 'Is my son ill?' he demanded harshly. It was the only viable reason he could supply for the utterly beaten way she looked.

A powerful surge of adrenalin flooded his bloodstream. He was already mentally organising his precious son's immediate removal to a private clinic, the attendance of the best paediatrician procurable.

The ensuing wave of bone-shaking relief weakened him when she stated dully, 'Torry's fit and well. He's teething again. That's all. He was awake most of the night, but he's sleeping peacefully now.'

Weakened him, but only for that panic-filled moment. Back in control, he ordered, 'Sit down. Before you fall over,' he added censoriously. Then, with icy cool, 'My business is principally with you.'

Sophie sank onto the sofa. The jelly-like state of her legs gave her no other option. He would see his son before he left, he'd stated, as was his right. When he woke. But after such a restless night Torry might sleep for hours! How would she endure it?

He joined her, the long fingers of his strong, beautifully crafted hands clicking open his slim leather briefcase. Remembering the way those hands had caressed her body made her swallow convulsively, sweat suddenly beading her short upper lip.

Not turning his dark head to her, he extracted a sheet of closely typed, heavy and ornately headed paper. His voice was clipped and formal as he explained, 'This document sets out the terms of your settlement. A lump sum for the purchase of a suitable home, and monthly payments to ensure you and my son want for nothing. It also sets out my rights. To see my son at regular, mutually convenient times, and later, when he reaches school age, to have him spend his holidays with me in Italy. There is much he will need to learn about his heritage. I have already signed in the presence of my lawyer, as you will see...'

His words were drowned out in the thunder of blood in her ears. This was how it was going to have to be. Seeing him at regular intervals, the pain of loving him savagely intensifying every time, and as the years went by watching the growing closeness between father and son, never able to be part of it.

She felt the coolness of the paper against her hands and struggled to pull herself together. She had known how it must be, she thought rawly. Now all she had to do was accept it. Put up with it and stop behaving like a fool.

Welcome to the real world, Sophie Lang!

Glancing down at the document—she supposed she was meant to sign it too—her eyes widened with horror at the size of the lump sum stated. Buy a suitable home? She could buy a couple of palaces with that amount, and still have some left over!

The rest of the type blurred beneath her suddenly hazy eyes.

'I don't need that much—'

Tearing his masochistic gaze from devouring her enchanting profile, Ettore bunched his hands into fists to stop them reaching for her, holding her to his heavily beating heart, keeping her there always, close to him, caring for her, loving her.

'What you do need is a massive dose of common sense,' he got out gruffly, hating to see her so pale and tired, as if all the life had been drained from her. 'You're obviously not taking proper care of yourself. You need to, for my son's sake. You look a wreck.'

The moment the brutal words were out he deeply regretted them. *Madonna diavola!* Her soft mouth was quivering now, those long blonde-tipped lashes fluttering, to keep back the moisture that threatened to spill down her marble-pale cheeks.

Fighting the instinctive need to enfold her in his arms, to comfort her, take back his words, tell her that she would always be heart-wrenchingly beautiful in his eyes, he took his fountain pen from the brief-case, uncapped it and slid it over the table towards her.

'If you will sign? The funds will be immediately available to you. I will need your bank details, of course. And I will have a copy of this document sent to you in a day or two.'

Then he would be out of here. It had been too soon—much too soon. This visit had been a crass mistake. He should have left everything in the hands of his lawyers. He had wanted to see her, had thought of nothing else since the day she had been driven to the airport. He'd thought he could handle it. But he couldn't. For the first time in his life he was up against something he couldn't cope with.

'Of course. Excuse me. Bank details,' she squawked.

Fired by the need to remove herself before she started howling her eyes out, Sophie shot to her feet and headed on unsteady limbs for the relative privacy of the kitchen, ignoring the pen.

Leaning against the sink, she let the tears she'd desperately held back gush. She knuckled her hands against her teeth to stifle the sobs that were building painfully in her throat. Once he had called her beautiful. Now she was a wreck. Well, she knew that, didn't she?

Too many sleepless nights—and only one of them down to a restless teething baby. Long sleepless hours tossing and turning in her brick-hard narrow bed, thinking of Ettore, missing him with every fibre of her body and soul. And she was unable to do more than pick at her food; the strain of trying to keep up a cheerful façade around her baby and Tim was wearing her down.

Vowing to pull herself together, to make herself get on with it and count her many blessings, she scrubbed her eyes with a fistful of kitchen roll and all but leapt out of her skin as that deep, velvety voice demanded, 'Why do you weep? Is Tim—' the name stuck in his craw but he got it out '—ill-treating you? If he is—'

The incisive warning of danger was a definite wake-up call. Turning quickly, her heart racing, she plastered what she hoped would pass for an incredulous smile on her mouth and tried for lightness. 'Of course not! Tim's been absolutely wonderful. He wouldn't ill treat a fly!' And trembled inside because filling the doorway, so gorgeous, so dark, so shiver-makingly brooding, he overpowered her senses. She had to make herself get over this, so she asked. 'And you? Have you got what you wanted? How is Cinzia?'

This was hurting, but she had to know. After that phone conversation with his jilted fiancée she had known that her own hopes of future happiness with this man were pretty well non-existent, so she really hadn't sacrificed anything, had she? 'Has she forgiven you?' she burbled, trying to sound sympathetic and hopeful at the same time.

'You talk in riddles. But on the subject of Cinzia there are things I have to tell you.' He stood aside, an imperious brow lifting. 'Come—this is not a pleasant place to be. I have a belated apology to make.'

About what? was Sophie's hectic question as she took a reluctant step towards him. Even if his moral behaviour had been decidedly iffy, he had been fair. He had offered to marry her, even breaking off with his high-status longstanding fiancée when he'd believed she might change her mind and grab his offer with both hands. And on her second refusal he had made eye-popping sums of money available to her. He'd even given up on his stated intention of being around full time for his son. She had to give him credit for that.

He didn't touch her as she slid past him in the doorway, although every inch of her heatedly wished he would—just one last time. She was like an addict, needing a fix regardless of the danger, she decided, loathing her weakness. He did that to her—always had done. Made her desire him, intoxicating every sense. Her awareness of him was sheer torture. And there were flags of bright colour on her pale cheeks as a brusque hand gesture motioned her to the sofa.

His dramatically handsome features had never looked so grim, and his velvet-smooth voice had never sounded so abrasive as he sat beside her, angled into the corner, and stated, 'From things said—small, unconnected pieces of information—I began to suspect I had misjudged you in the matter of the theft.'

'Well, bully for you!' Her sarcasm was edged with apathy. How she'd once craved to hear those words from him, the smallest inkling that he believed her. But that had been in the past. Now they didn't matter a toss.

Ettore gritted his teeth. He supposed he deserved that. That and much more punishment. He watched her swipe a lock of that glorious blonde hair away from her face and ploughed on, hating what he'd discovered, hating himself even more for ever believing the accusation of theft for a single moment.

'I had to have them confirmed before I spoke to you. I work with facts, not suppositions. You will remember the morning I left you early to drive to Florence?'

Sophie buttoned her lips and flatly refused to answer that! Of course she remembered! How could she forget how stupidly happy she'd been, how sure they could make marriage work? She didn't want to remember, but how the heck was she supposed to forget! She twisted her hands together in her lap and gave him a stubborn glare.

'I'll take that as a yes, shall I?' This was proving to be even more difficult than he'd imagined. 'Faced with what I had been able to put together, Cinzia confessed to having instructed her personal maid to put the diamond choker in your suitcase.'

He owed her this apology, but it would be truncated. Of necessity. He shouldn't have come. He needed out. As in right now. Loving her more than he'd believed possible, it was not a good idea to be here with her alone. It tried his mental and physical control to its outer limits.

It was Tim she wanted. Not him, he reminded himself with stark vehemence.

'I'm deeply sorry for doubting you.' He put the pen back in her hands and edged the document towards her.

She immediately dropped the pen back on the table. Ettore sighed edgily. A heavily voiced minimal apology wasn't good enough. He owed her more than that.

Biting the bullet, he went on flatly, 'My only defence is that, as I said, I always deal with facts—that is the way my mind works. The banker in me, I guess!' His feeble attempt at humour made no impression. He drew in a heavy breath and pressed on. 'When Cinzia first made that accusation I refused to believe a word of it. When the jewel was discovered in your suitcase I still did not want to believe. But it was a fact. I couldn't pretend any differently. And, wrongly, I translated your silence when the proof was revealed as guilt, though now I can understand you were in shock.'

An anger that was as unexpected as it was fierce and swift took hold of her. She recognised it as a form of release from the web of helpless yearning she had been unable to shake off ever since she'd left Tuscany, and accordingly she let rip.

'So a stilted apology for something that was un-forgivable makes everything all right, does it?' Sophie snapped, hands gripping her hands, as if she had every intention of breaking all her own fingers. 'I didn't know the wretched woman and she didn't know me—yet she got me thrown out of your sister's home in disgrace, humiliated, and you made sure I was blacklisted by the agency! And you—' Tears of rage glittered in her eyes. 'You still want to marry such a creature, even knowing what she's capable of! Well, I hope you'll be very happy!' And ignomini-ously she burst into tears.

Then found her clenched hands being gently prised apart, Ettore's long fingers stroking hers. 'Please don't cry.' He sounded hoarse.

'I can if I want to!' she howled, deep in the grip of childish fury. Sick of being a martyr, she yelled, 'She's deranged and spiteful, but she's got a top-notch pedigree and loads of money and mixes in the right circles—that's why you want to marry her! You don't love her, only what she stands for. If you did you wouldn't go around sleeping with the nearest willing female! And I really don't know how I can love such a creep!'

She snapped her mouth shut, her face turning bright crimson as she wished she could claw the re-vealing words back, and shrivelled in horrified si-lence as his fingers stilled on hers, then tightened, his voice rough round the edges as he commanded softly, 'Say that again.'

CHAPTER TWELVE

HER face burning with humiliation, Sophie wished the floor would open up and swallow her. What had she gone and said that for? What in heaven's name had possessed her? Too much raw emotion, she supposed, shrivelling up inside.

Those intelligent black eyes of his pierced her. He could see straight through her, and it made her feel so vulnerable and utterly, utterly stupid.

'Just forget it—'

As a response to his command it was totally pathetic, but the best she could think of right now. Somehow she had to put the lid on that line of questioning. Somehow!

Scrambling awkwardly to her feet, she avoided those too clever eyes and babbled, 'You'd like coffee while you're waiting? Or you could go and come back later, when Torry's awake, and—'

'Like an elephant, I never forget.' Two firm hands had moved to her waist, depositing her back on the sofa rather closer to him than she thought she could reasonably be expected to bear. Her heart was beating fast enough to choke her, and she knew her face was still glowing like a red traffic light.

She'd blurted something he couldn't possibly want to know, so why couldn't he brush it aside as she wanted him to? His hands were still clamped around her waist and beneath them her flesh burned and trembled, the old familiar spiral of desire squirming around her pelvis. Like everything else about her, she decided, her instinctive reaction to this one man was pathetic, and there was nothing she could do about it.

She had to say something to explain that verbal slip-up. Anything! Would *Only joking!* do? But her mouth had run dry. Her breath catching, she tried to moisten her lips with the tip of her tongue and risked a look at him between the tumbled, all-over-the-place wild strands of her hair.

He looked as if she'd just struck his face. Hurt, with a definite underlying layer of anger—or was that distaste? Of course, he would find her blurted admission about as welcome as a bad smell!

Back on the magical island, when she had first fallen fathoms-deep in love with him, they'd spoken words of love. He because it had prettied up raging animal lust, had been part of the game he must have played dozens of times in his privileged, sophisticated life. Doubtless he would have reasoned that she was playing the same game and knew the rules. And now her stupid words had alerted him to the fact that she'd meant it, and still loved him despite everything that had happened.

As a sophisticated member of the cream of Italian society he would think she was exactly what she was. An inexperienced fool whose natural habitat was cloud cuckoo land! Oh, why had she opened her big mouth and complicated an already fraught relationship?

'What are you trying to do, Sophie?' His hands dropped away. Was she deliberately trying to hurt him? Reject his offer of love and opt to return to her English lover, then turn round and torment him, talking of love? 'I want an answer,' he stated grittily.

She stole another upward glance, and the 'only joking' quip died in her throat. His beautiful mouth was drawn in a tight line, but the dark pools of his eyes were strangely vulnerable. And dismay claimed her when he pointed out the obvious.

'You chose to leave me and return to your lover. Now you tell me the very thing I've longed to hear! Payback time for past wrongs?'

Longed to hear? As if! Her expressive features clouded. If she tried to get to her feet and walk away he would pin her down again. Compromising, she shuffled to the far end of the sofa and pushed out, 'Tim's not my lover and never has been. He took me in out of the goodness of his heart. Torry and I had nowhere else to go. I've known him since I was about seven years old; he's my best friend's brother. And why on earth would you 'long' to hear me say I loved you? To boost your ego? I don't think it needs it, do you? It's already six times as big as a house.'

Brushing the insult aside, Ettore let his eyes track over her bristling figure, dressed in a thick check shirt and an old pair of jeans. He flinched inside as he recalled how she'd left everything he'd bought her behind at the villa. She'd wanted no reminders of him.

'Then why did you indulge in that long, cosy conversation when you believed me to be absent?' he questioned, his features rawly defined as he recalled the moment when all his hopes had died. 'A conversation that included your protestations that as I was your baby's father you had no choice but to agree to my demands but that you'd make everything all right. For him. Do you know how that made me feel? Two inches tall!'

About to yell *Good!*, Sophie swallowed the word and tipped her head on one side. Everything was beginning to look strangely out of kilter. In view of what she'd learned from his jilted fiancée, nothing made sense. She asked 'Why?'

'Why do you think?' he shot at her with scorn as he got restlessly to his feet.

Pacing the sparsely furnished room, he came to an abrupt halt in front of the window, with its uninspiring view of dustbins. 'I hate reminding myself, but I'd truly given you no option but to dance to my tune. Right from the beginning, still uneasily believing you were light-fingered, I had every intention of marrying you for our son's sake. My own, too,' he confessed raggedly. 'I was still crazy for you. Still in love with you, if I'm going to be completely honest. Though at that time I didn't admit it to myself.'

He stuffed his hands in the pockets of his immaculately tailored trousers and turned his back on her, taking, so it seemed, an inordinate interest in the neighbourhood dustbins. 'That telephone conversation, at least the part I overheard, brought home to me how unfair I was being. I did the only thing I could do. I offered you the choice of marrying me or returning here—to him. Loving you, I wanted—still want—you to be happy.'

Sophie's stomach looped the loop. Pressing her fingertips to her overheated temples, she tried to calm the churning muddle that passed for her mind and heaved herself onto her feet.

Crossing the room to stand directly behind him, wincing at the prospect of talking to that rigid broad back and deciding that she now knew exactly how Alice must have felt when she wandered into Wonderland, she swiftly inserted herself between him and the windowframe.

He didn't step back, away from her, but she did hear the ragged tug of his indrawn breath. She hadn't been hearing things, she staunchly impressed on herself. She had heard him say he loved her. But she didn't understand. It was driving her crazy!

He looked so remote, too. Clearly he wasn't into soul-baring. Typical man! How could he drop such an unexpected bombshell and then, in that superior male fashion, decide that he owed her no further explanation!

'Tim only phoned to find out if I was okay,' she bristled up at his tough-as-rock features. 'I'd promised to keep him up to speed but I forgot. And he was getting a load of hassle from his parents and my best friend—his sister—for allowing me to be what they'd decided was as good as kidnapped! So I was putting his mind at rest, promising to contact his folks and put the record straight, wasn't I?' she demanded fiercely, noting that not by so much as a flicker of an eyelash did he register that he was taking in a word she said. 'And because of a handful of overheard words you decided to give me and Torry our marching orders!'

Ettore took a backward step, putting space between them. Being this close to her was a severe strain on his self-control.

He had told her how he felt, but for all the good it had done he might have been reciting a chunk of the telephone directory. She had said nothing to explain her earlier blurted and—as he now had to deflatedly accept—patently untrue protestation of love. 'I did no such thing. I offered to marry you,' he reminded her tonelessly. 'You chose to turn me down.'

A response at last! But totally frustrating! Sophie wanted to shake him! Stepping closer—he wasn't going to back out of this—her breasts heaving with agitation, she shot out, 'I had no option, did I? I'd just had the lovely Cinzia bending my ear, accusing me of breaking up your beautiful longstanding engagement only that very morning. Pressing home the fact that you and she were the perfect couple but you felt duty-bound to marry me because I'd had your baby!'

She dragged in a heaving breath, horribly aware that she was in danger of losing it altogether—breaking down into a heap of frustrated misery. Because although he'd said he loved her he was obviously uninterested in sorting out the tangled strands of this messy eternal triangle. 'I was obviously standing in the way of your future happiness with your so-perfect life partner, so what else could I do?'

Ettore's brain clicked into gear. His heart took wing. His darling's head was downbent now, and a single silvery tear was trickling down the petal-soft skin of her cheek towards the corner of her lush, tremulous mouth. Taking immediate advantage of her obviously highly emotional state, he gathered her into his arms, one hand driving up to hold her head against his rapidly beating heart.

'Forget Cinzia. Put the wretched woman right out of your mind. You are the only woman I've ever truly loved,' he vowed thickly. 'Believe me.'

Sophie's heart jumped. She wanted to believe him with a desperation that was truly frightening. Wanted to wriggle ever closer to that strong male body, to be held, to be safe.

But the danger that she might be led again on the path to a fool's paradise and end up even more hurt, if that were possible, had her muttering against his perfectly tailored jacket, 'How can I believe that when up until a couple of weeks ago you had been planning to marry her? You've been engaged to the perfect Cinzia since the day you were born!' she exaggerated wildly, attempting to push him away as she became aware of the telltale hardening response of that beautiful male body.

'Virtually,' Ettore agreed with a resigned huff of amusement, and gathered her graceful body close to his again. He would never let her escape him, not while they were both breathing. To post his intentions, he tipped her head back and found her mouth hungrily, and Sophie, all her instincts for self-preservation thrust heedlessly onto the back burner, responded with passionate exuberance, melting into him until, lifting his dark head, he said shakily, 'Now deny that you love me.'

She shook her head, her mouth burning from his kisses, her body aching for more. 'I can't,' she assured him breathily. 'I have loved you since—since the island.'

His dark eyes flared with triumph. 'Me too.' His voice was soft, compellingly so. 'Come, I need to clear your beautiful head of any lingering misconceptions before I take you back to our home in Italy. Because, my only love, whether or not you agree to be my wife, I am never going to let you out of my sight again.' He took both her hands in his and led her to the sofa, releasing fingers that would have clung with a self-deprecating smile. 'If we are touching I will not be responsible for my actions.'

A scenario that set Sophie craving him even more, and her eyes were hazy with her need for him as he stated grimly, 'Don't look at me like that! You will tempt me into forgetting my own name—never mind what I have to say to you.'

'Which is?' Sophie lowered her head demurely, but she was smiling. She had never felt so sure of herself, of her feminine power, as she did at this moment.

Shifting at the other end of the sofa, as if he were experiencing a few anatomical difficulties, Ettore said gruffly, 'You were right. I was betrothed to Cinzia di Barsini when I was barely out of my teens. An arrangement instigated by both sets of parents. Highly advantageous to all parties concerned. The done thing in the circles we moved in. We didn't love each other, but it was a highly suitable match. And neither of us was in the least hurry to set a marriage date.'

His wide shoulders lifted dismissively. Then, his

glittering eyes intent on hers, he vowed, 'Even before I fell in love with you I had decided that on my return to Florence I would terminate the engagement. With honour, I knew it had to be done in person. Regardless of our families' desire, I just knew there had to be more to marriage than the consolidation of two great fortunes. Even so, my falling in love with you—for the first time in my life I understood what love meant—led to a delay in returning to Florence. I told Cinzia that the engagement was off, and confessed I'd found you and that you were my life, on the night of Flavia's party—the first opportunity I had. She tried to talk me out of it—I didn't know at that time that her father was getting into troubled financial waters—and when, finally, I was free, I tried to find you—only to have Flavia tell me that you had gone early to bed because you felt unwell.'

'Cinzia had told me that you and she were shortly to be married,' Sophie put in. 'Your sister confirmed it. I was in shock. I'd never felt so hurt—so betrayed.'

Pale-faced, she shuddered at the memory, and Ettore, good intentions blown in the wind, moved to her side and gathered her in his arms, begging hoarsely, 'Will you ever be able to forgive me for what happened? Will you try? Cinzia did an evil thing. Realising that none of her arguments could sway me, she decided to blacken you in my eyes, brand you a thief. And to my shame I believed the evidence. You were in shock. I had no idea at the time that you'd been told of my engagement. And those two shocks in swift succession had rendered you speechless in your own defence. I am as culpable as she!'

Staunchly resisting the incredibly strong impulse to tell him she would forgive him anything and everything, Sophie got out shakily, 'And you went back to being engaged to her again?'

'Yes.' He looked devastated. 'I was beyond caring!'

He vented what she took to be a blistering oath in his own language.

'As far as I knew at that dreadful time, the woman I'd loved as I'd never loved anyone in my entire life had turned out to be a common thief. She had never loved me, only what she'd thought she could get from me.'

His anguished frown brought his dark brows together. 'Please, my darling, try to understand—I fully intended to return to London when you did and beg you to marry me. I said nothing of this to you, though I ached to do so, believing it was my duty to break off with Cinzia before I made my future intentions to you clear. Therefore I thought—unforgivably—that as I had made no move to give you a pay-off for services rendered on the island, you'd decided to help yourself to what you thought was owed to you. So,' he said with heavy regret, 'I again fell in with everyone's wishes. I was beyond caring about my future. Threw myself into my work to the exclusion of all else. Then I saw you again in London. With our child.'

His thick lashes swept down as he drew in a shuddering breath and Sophie, her heart so full of love it positively ached, raised her hands to run the tips of her fingers over the fascinating planes of his face. 'You frightened me then,' she confessed lovingly. 'I thought you would move heaven and earth to take Torry from me. You still thought I was a thief, and I believed you were responsible for getting me black-listed.'

'That was Cinzia.' He lifted his head and his mouth twisted wryly. 'Against my wishes. And for what it's worth I would never have separated you from our baby. You need each other. But I needed you, too, and threats were the only way I could think of to keep you with me.'

'Don't beat yourself up about it! I'm glad you did.' And to drive her point home she raised her head and touched her lips to his.

His response was masterfully immediate, his mouth devouring hers, his tongue delving with explicit provocation between her lips, setting up a wild conflagration inside her, and it was a long time before Sophie found herself being thrust gently back against the cushions, out of breath and aching for more.

'I'm rapidly losing all control,' Ettore husked, under visible strain. 'But when we again make love it's going to be perfect for us.' His firm mouth curved wryly. 'Not in this place, with a hungry baby liable to disturb us at any moment.'

Then, smiling that utterly charismatic smile of his, always to be relied upon to melt every last bone in her body, he softly pushed the tangled strands of her hair away from her face with strong, gentle hands and confided, 'If you remember, I left you at the villa at almost the same time we'd arrived there. I was in haste to end my sterile relationship with Cinzia once and for all, and to tell my mother and my sister that I had a beautiful baby son and intended to marry his beautiful mother.'

Colour slashed over his fabulously sculpted cheekbones as he said tightly, 'Cinzia obviously led you to believe that I had only broken with her on that second time I visited her. Not true. I'd already suspected she was behind the so-called theft for mercenary reasons of her own. I went to confront her. Her father is now facing bankruptcy. It has been coming on for some time, it appears. She was desperate to hold on to me, and my wealth, hence her scheme to blacken your character.'

His eyes intent on her pale features, he grated, 'My suspicions confirmed, I came back to you. Desperate to seek your forgiveness and to ask you again to be my wife, to go down on my knees, if necessary, and beg you to try to love me as I love you. But Cinzia, even though she'd known for some time that our engagement was over, had to put her poison in. I should have expected it. I'd made her confess to her malicious behaviour, and I'd told her exactly what I thought of her. That, together with the bitter knowledge that she would never now happily enjoy the wealth I could provide, must have led her to decide that you, the woman she knew I loved, wouldn't be happy either.'

He swallowed hard, his eyes holding hers. 'You will marry me?'

Suppressing the wicked impulse to say, *Try your very best to persuade me!*, she wrapped her arms around his neck, her heart in her eyes as she breathed,

'Yes, please. Tomorrow. Today. This minute!' and watched sheer joy light his wonderful eyes.

At the same moment they heard Tim's key in the door.

Sophie stilled as her friend clumped into the room, calling out, 'You okay, Soph? I left work early to check—that guy was here—'

He broke off as Ettore rose to his feet, six feet plus of lean, powerful masculinity. For a moment the two men stared at each other. Two splashes of red colour appeared on Tim's winter-pale cheeks and Sophie held her breath, fearing some kind of confrontation in which poor Tim would come off decidedly second best. Then Ettore grinned.

'Thank you for looking after her for me. Sophie's told me how good you've been.' He turned to her, his dark eyes alight. 'Sophie, you have something to tell your friend?'

Liberated from her frozen stance, she leapt to her feet and tucked her hand beneath Ettore's arm, her face radiant. 'We are to be married in—' A questioning look at the man she adored.

'In four weeks,' he supplied. 'I'd like it to be very much sooner, but if the love of my life is to have the wedding she deserves it cannot be arranged much earlier.' He dragged his gaze from his darling's vibrant features and turned again to the younger man. 'We would both be happy if you could attend, as one of Sophie's oldest friends and part of the closest thing she has to a family.'

'And Tina and her husband, if they can manage it. And your parents, of course. They'll be back from Canada by then,' Sophie put in, her euphoria making her babble, and her relief when Tim broke into a huge grin making her feel light-headed.

He shrugged out of his coat and advanced to where they stood, holding out a hand, which Ettore took, returning the younger man's hearty handshake.

'Congrats, and all that!' His blue eyes twinkled at Sophie. 'I seem to have spent the best part of my growing up years looking out for my kid sister and Sophie. Tina's safely married, and now you'll be taking Sophie off my hands! Not to mention getting my folks off my back!'

'In that case,' she put in, beaming from ear to ear, 'you will be happy to give me away!'

'You bet!' He ruffled her hair, grinning. 'It would be an honour. Now, who wants a sandwich? I'm starving. Corned beef? Or corned beef?'

Not waiting for a reply, he made for the kitchen.

Sophie said, 'I'm so happy I could burst! Will you always love me? Tell me how much.'

Ettore gave her an adoring look. 'More than my life, and I have a lifetime to prove it.' He tipped his head on one side. 'Do you hear something?'

'Our son is waking. Come.' She tugged at his hand. 'He has missed you.'

Torry was lying on his back, kicking his legs in the air and gurgling. The moment two doting parents bent over him he bestowed a chortling laugh, and Ettore said proudly, 'He has another tooth!' as if it were the greatest achievement the world had ever seen. He bent to pick him up, hoisting the ecstatic baby in the air and finally bestowing kisses on both chubby cheeks before putting him in Sophie's arms, enfolding them both in his own, and vowing, 'My family—I am the luckiest man in the universe!'

Four weeks later

It had been a perfect wedding. Handing Sophie, still in her wedding finery, into the car, for the drive back to their villa, Ettore carefully tucked what seemed like acres of creamy wild silk around her dainty feet and told her huskily, 'You are so beautiful I can't take my eyes off you!'

He brushed the short filmy veil away from her face and kissed her lingeringly, and Sophie felt her breasts tighten beneath her close-fitting bodice. She placed her hands on his wide, impeccably clad shoulders and murmured breathlessly, 'If you don't stop kissing me we will both disgrace ourselves in public!' and earned herself a wry grin of total understanding as his hands slid from her tiny waist, where they'd been creating havoc, and he drew himself upright.

Driving away at last, to cheers, laughter and the good wishes of the assembled guests, Sophie spared a special backward glance to where Torry, clad in a miniature sailor suit and looking completely adorable, was waving his chubby arms haphazardly in the air, firmly held by his doting grandmother.

'You were right. He won't miss us, just for this one special night,' she admitted, devouring Ettore's startlingly handsome profile.

'Of course. Aren't I always?' He spared her one of his slashing grins. 'Everyone adores him, and Minette will make sure he doesn't get too spoiled or over-excited, and tomorrow she and our son will be driven home to us and our family life will begin.' A tanned hand rested briefly on her knee as he assured her, 'I'm looking forward to that more than I can tell you. And next week the four of us will travel to my villa in the hills behind Amalfi for a summer-long honeymoon. Where Minette will take charge of Torry when we want to be alone. But tonight, my darling, is for the two of us. I need you all to myself.'

Suffused with pleasure and mounting anticipation, Sophie relaxed back in the comfort of the leather upholstery. They would be completely alone. Indeed, all the staff had attended the wedding and would be travelling back in convoy with their baby and his nanny tomorrow.

This night was just for the two of them.

Blissfully, her mind wandered back over the past four weeks. It had been hectic.

Flavia had welcomed her with hugs and kisses. 'I'm so glad that horrid misunderstanding has been cleared up. Oh, that dreadful, evil woman—I could cheerfully strangle her! I knew why the engagement had been arranged, but I never liked the idea. She would have made him miserable. But now we will talk of her no more—just concentrate on how happy you will make Ettore. I have never seen him look happier than he is now—I can tell you, since you left us in those terrible circumstances he turned into a workaholic with such a bleak face!'

Flavia and her husband had insisted that she be married from their home in Florence—insisted, too, that the English contingent stayed there over the wedding period.

Meeting Ettore's mother for the first time had been scary. But she'd greeted Sophie with warmth, demanded to be addressed as Madre, and the elegant elderly woman had fallen immediate captive to baby Torry—who, she'd declared, was the image of Ettore at that tender age.

Choosing her wedding gown and conferring with Flavia, who had stated that the reception had to be fit for royalty, had left her little time to miss Ettore himself, who had been hard at work at head office, making sure that everything was in order before he took an extended honeymoon, and had ensured that the time they did manage to spend together was doubly precious.

The journey passed swiftly, and Sophie came out of her happy reverie when Ettore cut the engine and announced, 'Home.'

Staring up at the beautiful villa, at the evening sun setting beyond the Tuscan hills, Sophie felt her eyes mist with pure happiness. She closed them in bliss as he helped her from the car and lifted her in his strong arms to carry her over the threshold, her arms twined lovingly around his neck, her face close to his, feeling his featherlight kisses.

She only opened them again when he slid her to her feet in the immense hall, and she let out a squeak of joyful disbelief.

In the centre stood Nanny Hopkins's pram, looking as if it had been made only yesterday. Black coachwork gleaming, chrome glittering, fresh, pristine, luxurious white padding on the interior.

'For you, my darling wife,' Ettore murmured, running a finger over her open mouth, circling her lips.

'I gathered it had sentimental value, so I arranged for it to be collected from where it had been abandoned in Tim's hallway, and had it completely renovated and shipped over when all was as good as new.'

His hands circled her tiny waist and his dark head dipped to claim her soft mouth with passionately demanding lips, eventually coming up for air to say in that sexy drawl of his, 'Our son is too big to need it. But one day there may be another tiny baby to enjoy riding in such Rolls Royce-type luxury, don't you think?'

Sophie's heart swelled within her bosom, her eyes misting over again. That this super-fastidious guy, the man who had offloaded the old pram onto a charity shop, deeming the nearest skip the only proper place for it, had not only got it back for her but, at surely great expense, had had it made as good as new made her go all mushy inside. She slid her arms around his neck and her voice sounded smoky as she focused on his melting eyes and answered, 'At least two more to enjoy it.' The tip of her pink tongue came out to circle her lush lips. 'I guess we should start doing something about it.'

With a thrilling growl of masculine approval, Ettore swept her up in his arms. 'That, my dearest love, is the best idea I've heard in a long while.' And he carried her in haste towards the sweeping staircase.

Introducing a brand-new miniseries

FOR *Love* OR MONEY

This is romance on the red carpet…

For Love or Money is the ultimate reading experience
for the reader who has a taste for tales of wealth and
celebrity and the accompanying gossip and scandal!

Look out for the special covers
on these upcoming titles:

Coming in September:

EXPOSED: THE SHEIKH'S MISTRESS
by *Sharon Kendrick* #2488

As the respected ruler of a desert kingdom, Sheikh Hashim
Al Aswad must marry a suitable bride of impeccable virtue.
He previously left Sienna Baker when her past was exposed—
he saw the photos to prove it! But what is the truth behind
Sienna's scandal? And with passion between them this hot
will he be able to walk away…?

Coming soon:

HIS ONE-NIGHT MISTRESS
by Sandra Marton #2494

SALE OR RETURN BRIDE
by Sarah Morgan #2500

HARLEQUIN®
Presents~

Seduction and Passion Guaranteed!

www.eHarlequin.com

HPTSM

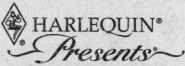

WIVES *Wanted!*

When a wealthy man wants a wife,
he doesn't always follow the rules!

Welcome to

Miranda Lee's

stunning, sexy new trilogy.

Meet Richard, Reece and Mike, three Sydney
millionaires with a mission—they all want to get
married...but none wants to fall in love!

Coming in August 2005:

BOUGHT: ONE BRIDE #2483

Richard's story: His money can buy him anything
he wants...and he wants a wife!

Coming in September:

THE TYCOON'S TROPHY WIFE #2489

Reece's story: She was everything he wanted in a wife...
until he fell in love with her!

Coming in October:

A SCANDALOUS MARRIAGE #2496

Mike's story: He married her for money—
her beauty was a bonus!

Coming Next Month

THE BEST HAS JUST GOTTEN BETTER!

#2493 THE BRAZILIAN'S BLACKMAILED BRIDE Michelle Reid
The Ramirez Brides
Anton Luis Scott-Lee is going to marry Cristina Marques. She rejected him years ago and his payback will be sweet: she will be at Luis's bidding—bought and paid for! But Luis will find that his bride can't or *won't* fulfill all of her wedding vows....

#2494 HIS ONE-NIGHT MISTRESS Sandra Field
For Love or Money
Lia knew that billionaire businessman Seth could destroy her glittering career. But he was so attractive that she succumbed to him—for one night! Eight years on, Lia's successful. When he sees Lia in the papers, Seth finds that he has a love child, and is determined to get her back!

#2495 EXPECTING THE PLAYBOY'S HEIR Penny Jordan
Jet-Set Wives
American billionaire Silas Carter has no plans for love—he wants a practical marriage. So he only proposes to beautiful Julia Fellowes as a ruse to get rid of her lecherous boss and to indulge in a hot affair—or that's what he lets her think!

#2496 A SCANDALOUS MARRIAGE Miranda Lee
Wives Wanted
Sydney entrepreneur Mike Stone has a month to get married—or he'll lose a business deal worth billions. Natalie Fairlane, owner of the *Wives Wanted* introduction agency, is appalled by his proposition! But the exorbitant fee Mike is offering for a temporary wife is *very* tempting...!

#2497 THE GREEK'S ULTIMATE REVENGE Julia James
The Greek Tycoons
Greek tycoon Nikos Kyriades wants revenge—and he's planned it. He'll treat Janine Fareham to a spectacular seduction, and he has two weeks on a sunny Greek island to do it. If Janine discovers she's a pawn in his game, Nikos knows she'll leave—but it's a risk he'll take to have her in his bed!

#2498 THE SPANIARD'S INCONVENIENT WIFE Kate Walker
The Alcolar Family
Ramon Dario desperately wants the Medrano company—but there is a condition: he must marry the notorious Estrella Medrano! Ramon will not be forced into marriage, but when he sees the gorgeous Estrella, he starts to change his mind....